ECHOED HEARTBEATS

CIN MEDLEY

MED'S PUB
PUBLISHING

CIN MEDLEY

The characters in this book are not real people. They have been made up. They are by no means related to or pertain to anyone.
This material is copyrighted. No portion of this book may be used without written permission from the publisher.

Published by: Med's Pub Publishing
Copyright © 2020 Cin Medley
All Rights Reserved
ISBN-13: 978-1-7342690-3-1
Cover Design by Amanda Walker
P.A. and Design Services
Edited and Proofed by Kendra Gaither at Kendra's
Editing and Book Services
Formatting by Med's Pub Publishing

It is said some lives are linked across time.
Connected by an ancient calling that echoes through the ages.
Destiny
Prince of Persia~The Sands of Time

What is time? It's a form of measurement used to sequence events, to compare the duration of events or the intervals between them. The past, present, and future.

But what if the measurement of time doesn't exist between the past, the present, and the future?

What if the past has a way of becoming the present? Or if the present can then become the future?

A story as old as time, a story of the past that has become the present. Two old souls that existed in the past, loved in the past, have now become the present and live for the future of what will be.

One look to intertwine in the present what was connected in the past, a great and powerful connection of love. Two strangers find themselves in a measurement of time, the connection of old souls.

Love stands the test of time. It lasts beyond our physical world, or, at least, we like to think it does.

CHAPTER ONE

JAYCEN

"You know what, Sherry? What the fuck do I pay you so much money for? Get the fucker under control, or he's out. I will buy out his fucking contract and drop his ass. His drinking is out of control and destroying hotel rooms went out in the fucking eighties."

"Jay, I've tried numerous times. He had a bad break-up, and now, he just wants to drink and cry."

I couldn't stop my humorless laugh. "I just went through a break-up, and you don't see me getting drunk and crying, destroying everything I see." I couldn't help but smile. I did exactly that when Ashley cheated on me. Fucking bitch fucked some guy in our bed. In my bed. I think taking a knife to it and shredding it while I was drunk was exactly what this fucking low life Ted Nicks did. More than once. "He's got a week. You've got a week. I'm not fucking around anymore. This bastard is costing me more money than he is making me. One week, Sherry, or he's gone."

"Okay, I'll let him know. Thanks, Jay."

"Don't thank me. Your ass is on the line, as well. This is the third client you've lost control over."

"Thanks for the reminder."

I couldn't help but chuckle. I liked Sherry, but she'd been slacking in her job of finding me talent, and the talent she did bring me were fucking losers. I disconnected the call; I had no desire to talk to her anymore. Pushing out of my chair, I walked to the window to look down at the great city of Chicago from my ivory tower. It's what Ashley said as she dressed, that I thought myself untouchable in my ivory tower and that I expected everyone to bow at my feet. I was a bastard at times, but you had to be tough in order to make it in the music business. I owned the fourth largest recording company in the country.

My cell vibrated on my desk, but I really didn't want to answer it. I was pretty sure it'd be Ashley again, begging me to forgive her. No way was that ever going to happen. I may have been an arrogant son of a bitch, but I didn't think it was unrealistic to ask for complete monogamy from a person. I worked unreasonable hours, sure. I was out constantly, scouting for new acts, but she never wanted to come with me.

It still burned deep inside, walking into my bedroom at three in the morning to find some guy on top of her, fucking her brains out. I nearly killed the guy, but then I realized it wasn't his fault. Ashley had always been a very beautiful woman, and I'd fucked her while she was with someone else. Closing my eyes, I could see her perfect fucking body; I remember that night like it was last night. She was wearing a stunning red dress with heels that made her legs go on forever. Fuck, she looked good in stilettos and nothing else but her painted red mouth. My cock got hard just thinking about smearing her lipstick all over her face with my kiss.

My phone vibrated again. As I turned, I saw Caden's goofy ass photo he put in my phone. He lived a few doors down from me when we were growing up. When I was the new kid, he defended me to the schoolyard bully who wanted to kill me, and we'd been friends ever since.

"What do you want, lowlife?" I barked into the phone.

"Fuck you, asshole." We laughed. "Listen, I wanted to remind you about tonight."

I closed my eyes. *Fuck, I don't want to do this.* "Listen, man, do I have to do this? Can't I just send one of my agents?"

"Listen, shithead, we've been friends for a long time. When have I ever asked you to do me a favor?"

"All the fucking time. I have a business to run."

"Exactly, and I think these guys might be your next find. I swear to you they are good. Just go listen to them, have a drink or two, and unwind. Ever since that bitch ripped your heart out, you've been sulking around."

"Fuck off, asshole. Tell me if you walked into your house and found your girlfriend fucking some guy you wouldn't be destroyed."

Caden laughed. "See, that's the difference between you and me. I know how to keep my woman happy in bed."

I couldn't contain my laughter. "I've seen your dick, asshole. Your mini-sausage has nothing on my salami."

Caden was laughing. "Perhaps, but it's not the size of the ship; it's the motion of the ocean."

"Fucker. What time and where? I swear, if they suck, I am going to post naked pictures of you at the reception."

"They don't suck. Do you think I'd have a sucky band at my wedding? Don't answer that. They go on at eight, play until midnight. The bar is called The Jewel, and the band is The Vibe."

The Jewel was a pretty upscale place. I supposed I should go. He was my best friend, and I am the best man at his wedding. "Fine, fucker. I'll call you tomorrow and let you know what I think."

"Thanks, man. I've got to run into a meeting."

I disconnected the call and stood to look out the window. I loved this city; it held many memories. Grabbing my jacket, I headed out. "Heidi, can you find me a real estate agent?"

"Of course."

"Give them my cell. I need to move."

Walking to the elevator, I felt a weight lift from my shoulders, but as it seemed to go with my life, when the doors opened, Ashley walked out. "What the fuck?" I mumbled. She stood there looking at me, her eyes puffy and red. She had been crying. I didn't really give a shit. I leaned in and, in probably the most hateful voice I'd ever heard come out of my mouth, said, "Get the fuck out of my building."

"Jay," she whispered as she recoiled away from me. "Please."

Shaking my head, I walked into the elevator and pushed the button to the garage. I was going to blow up, and my office wasn't the place to do it. My eyes bore into hers, so full of hate and anger like I'd never known. When I caught my father with his secretary all those years ago, I thought I knew anger then, but today, it was multiplied by a million easy. As the doors closed, I was so sure she would just disappear, but not a chance. Her hand slipped through the crack in the doors, holding it open. I almost wished the doors would have crushed her perfectly manicured fingers, but they didn't. Fuckers were spring-loaded with a sensor to open when something touched them.

She stepped in before I could tell her to get the fuck out, and the doors closed us in the too-small box. She stood directly in front of me, looking at me. She was wearing the fifteen-hundred-dollar coat I bought her. "Jay, please, can't we just talk about this?"

"In three years, I never cheated on you. So many women tried, but I walked away. Why? Because I loved you. I wanted only you." I chuckled. "I was so blinded by you. What a fucking joke. You made a fucking fool out of me, saying you loved me and then fucking men behind my back. I gave you everything."

"You did, Jay, and I'm so sorry. I was lonely. I wanted you, but you weren't there."

"Fuck you, Ash. Fuck you. We're over. We probably should have ended it a long time ago. Just get the rest of your shit out of my apartment. I'm selling it. I can't live there anymore; I can't live in a space I shared with a slut. You're just a whore who fucked me for my money. Such a fool I was. Never again."

The doors opened, and I moved around her, fury blowing through my body. If a human could see red, that would be the color in my vision. She reached out, grabbing hold of my suit jacket. "Jay, please. I'm pregnant."

Ripping my arm away from her, I laughed. I knew I couldn't have children. I never wanted them. I never wanted them to suffer the emotional turmoil I did because people couldn't stay true to one another. She was living proof of that. "If you are, then it's someone else's."

"No, Jay, it's yours," she cried.

I walked away and kept walking. I could hear the clicking of her shoes echoing across the concrete. I used to smile at that sound, knowing that soon after, I would be buried deep inside of her beautiful body. But now it just made my skin crawl.

"Jay, stop," she yelled.

I didn't. I couldn't. I was still in shock that I'd allowed myself to be pulled into this bitch's game. Now, she was trying to convince me that I'd fathered her unborn child. When I reached the car, my driver got out, but I shook my head at him and opened the back door. She put her hand on my arm, and my eyes drifted down to see her blood-red nails. I could remember how fantastic they'd felt when she would drag them down my back just before I fucking released.

"Why won't you talk to me? Why won't you believe me?"

She whimpered when I spun around to look at her lying, pathetic face. I got maybe an inch from it. "You are a fucking lying little slut. You cheated on me, fucked a man, or numerous men in our bed, the bed we shared. It's not my fucking spawn, Ash. I can't have children. Get. The. Fuck. Away. From. Me."

I turned and got in the car, slamming the door. My driver pulled away. Hopefully, it would be the last time I saw the bitch, but somehow, I knew it wouldn't be. She knew the ride she'd had, and she knew she'd fucked up. I would have given her the world and not thought twice about it. God, I wanted to punch something, someone. I needed to work out.

"Take me to the gym," I barked at my driver. It wasn't his fault that she was a whore.

When I walked out of the locker room, I was ready to get in the ring. Most of these guys were good, but I needed to fight with someone better. I needed to beat the shit out of someone or have the shit beat out of me. Spotting my trainer, Rudy, I headed over to him.

"Hey, Jay. Come to beat up my guys again?" He laughed.

"Actually, I was hoping for a more substantial opponent. Maybe someone with a bit more grit." I knew what I was asking, but I needed to give everything I had. I needed to find a way to rein in my anger, this absolute, all-encompassing rage. I wanted to hit her. I wanted to slam her against the wall for taking the love I gave her and so carelessly disregarding it, throwing it in my face. This is the reason I never wanted to do relationships before. I made the mistake of thinking she was different, made the mistake of thinking she was the one. The more I thought about the ring in my safe, the angrier I became.

Rudy laughed at me. "I've got someone to challenge you, but you've got to promise not to hurt him too badly. He has a fight coming up soon. You would be a good match for him." Leaning in, he added, "He may just give you a beat down."

"Good, that's just what I'm looking for."

If Rudy was fixing me up with one of his fighters, I knew I was about to get my ass kicked, but it didn't matter. I could give as good as I could take it. I watched as the cut-man taped my hands and fixed my gloves.

As Rudy's fighter walked over, I realized the guy was really big. But as full of rage as I was, he couldn't intimidate me. Rudy climbed in, and we began. After the first round, I could feel the buzz in my jaw. He had some power, but I gave as good as I got. After round two, I had a small cut on my eyebrow, but my rage was still going.

I closed my eyes, seeing her legs wrapped around that bastard. When I stood from my corner, we got back to it. I kept seeing the fucker's face when I turned on the light, her mouth in that ever so familiar O as she came undone. My left hit him in the jaw. I swung my right, connecting with his gut, and he bent slightly. Bringing my left up, I took him down. He flew back, his feet moving, and down he went to the mat.

"Come on!" I yelled at him. "Get up."

Rudy came over, pushing me back. "What the hell, Jay?"

I stood with a smirk on my face, the blood from the gash on my brow dripping on my cheek. Rudy snapped some smelling salts, waving them under my opponent's nose.

The guy sat up. "What the fuck?" He looked at me. "Who the hell are you?"

I just stood there looking at him as I pulled off my glove. "Jaycen Ashford."

He bumped fists with me. "You fight?"

I chuckled. "No, just a hobby."

He turned to Rudy. "I've never been knocked out. You should sign this guy."

Knowing he had never been taken down before felt good, but the rage still burned inside of me. The cut-man made me sit while he tended to my cut. "I don't think you'll need stitches. That was a hell of a left hook."

I was too pissed off to take the compliment, and when he finished, I went and got dressed. Just sitting on the bench in my slacks, with my head down, I felt like I was going to drown in my rage. I'm pretty sure I was still in love with that bitch. I knew I needed to get to the doctor and get a test, then stop and get some fucking condoms. I needed to fuck someone, anyone.

On my way out the door, Rudy approached me. "You sure you don't want to box?"

"No, thanks. It's just a hobby."

"Well, if you change your mind, I'm here."

Nodding, I walked out and got in my car. "I need you to take me to the doctor's office, the one on Michigan."

"Not a problem, sir."

With my eyes closed, I slumped my body down in the seat, laying my head back. Fuck, I wanted to fucking come. Beating the shit out of that guy wasn't enough. Maybe fucking the hell out of someone would help.

I wasn't aware the car had stopped. "Sir, we're here."

Leaning against the reception window, I said softly to the receptionist, "I need to see the doctor."

When she picked up her head, I could see the blush spread across her cheeks. "I'm sorry, but we don't have any openings, Mr.?"

I smiled. "Just tell Dr. Stevens that Jay is here to see him, please."

She swallowed hard. Chuckling, I walked over and sat down. Less than five minutes later, Alexander came out. "Jay, come on back." I stood, buttoning my jacket, then couldn't resist smiling at the receptionist as I walked by. "You need to stop swooning my girls."

I laughed. "Listen, I need to be tested. Fucking Ashley was cheating on me."

"Wow. No shit? I'm sorry, man." He patted me on the back. I hated that shit. I wasn't a fucking dog.

"When I walked in, the guy jumped off her, and he wasn't wearing a fucking condom, so I need to make sure she didn't give me something. I hate wearing fucking condoms, and until you give me a clean bill of health, I have to. I also need to make sure I'm still shooting blanks."

He laughed at me. "You know, you're the only man I know who fucks so freely. I would be scared shitless of catching something."

"Yeah, well, I've been fucking one chick for the past three years. Well, her and probably five other guys."

"I'm sorry, man. I know you loved her. Didn't you go ring shopping?"

"Yep. Good thing I never married her. She would be taking me to court right about now. Why can't I find a nice girl like Alice?" Alice was Alex's wife, who he had met in med school at Yale. We'd all been friends since then.

"One day, when you least expect it. Besides, I really don't think you're ready for that yet. You work way too hard and are never around. Hell, I was lucky you made it to my wedding, remember?"

It's a day I would never forget. I literally ran into the church two minutes before the bride walked down the aisle, and I was the best man. "Yeah, but that was one hell of a bachelor party. I struggled all day to not throw up."

We laughed, and he stood by as a nurse drew my blood. "Listen, why don't you come over for dinner tonight? I'm sure Alice would be glad to see you."

"I wish, but I promised Caden I would check out this band. He swears they are the next big thing. Maybe over the weekend. I'll call you."

"Sounds like a plan. I'll call Caden and see if they are busy."

I could do that. Something to get me out of that fucking apartment. I was so sick of the place. On my way out, after giving the nurse my sperm sample, my phone rang.

"Jaycen Ashford."

"Mr. Ashford, my name is Stella Michaels. Your secretary gave me this number. She said you were looking for a new apartment."

"She would be correct, the sooner, the better, and I would like to sell the one I own now." I gave her the details of where I lived and what I was looking for and where. She informed me that she would get back to me in a few days. Until then, I was going home to pack and planned on staying at a hotel.

I called Heidi and had her book me into the Lake Suite at the Peninsula downtown. I'd put rockers up there, the ones that knew how to be adults, so I knew the place was nice. I'd stay there for a while.

CHAPTER TWO

GWYN

Looking out the window at the parking lot, I shook my head. I just didn't want to do this. I hated singing in public. *Fuck!* I wanted to scream when my sister asked me to do this for her. If she wasn't my big sister, I would have told her no, but she always had a way of making me do things I didn't want, or things that scared the shit out of me.

I only hoped that the song we wrote for her was good enough. My eyes darted around at the crowd now forming. I was better behind the camera, hiding while I exposed the beauty in others, the beauty in life. My prints had been doing well, well enough to afford the travel. Well enough to do this. My eyes drifted to the seat next to me, where a copy of Time magazine laid with one of my photographs on the front. It was a huge honor, not to mention a huge paycheck for them to choose my photo. Looking at my watch, I saw it was nearly time to go in. Kyle and the guys had worked so hard to get here, to get this gig at The Jewel. In a sense, if it meant they got a recording contract, it would be great for them. But they did all right. A bus tour around the Midwest wasn't a shabby deal. If they only knew.

Looking up, I could see the bus from my seat. The guys filtered out, having one last smoke, one last drink before going on stage. My hand sat on the door handle, frozen there, unable to pull up. I just didn't want to do this. I'd promised Kyle I would shoot them, so they had some good promo pics.

Kyle saw me and started toward my car. "Fuck. Here we go." I smiled as he drew closer, forcing my hand to pull the door handle, not sure this is what I wanted to be doing. The repercussions to this night would be horrendous, but a promise is a promise, and I needed to practice the song. I shouldn't care what Gavin had to say. I mean, I did leave him the last time he hit me, and that was months ago. The bastard still thought he owned me, though, and showed up every now and then to cause nothing but problems for me. Last time, I ended up with a few bruised ribs, along with multiple bruises all over my body. Taking self-defense had helped me to fight back.

Opening the door, I felt a chill in the air, which was weird considering it was June. Kyle smiled at me. "You ready?"

I smiled my best smile. "Not really, but I need to practice. I need to know if this song is any good. But taking the pictures, not a problem."

"We've got a great set lined up, so the crowd should be ready when you come up. After our break, you're on."

I looked around, taking in all the cars and people in the parking lot. Something wasn't right. Something felt horribly wrong here.

"You all right?"

"Kyle, when I leave tonight, can you and the guys walk me to my car?"

His eyes immediately scanned the lot. "I won't let him hurt you again. Did you tell your father about what he's been doing? About him stalking you, hurting you?"

He wanted me to tell, but I couldn't. My father knew; he just pretended not to. It would only make it worse if I forced him to acknowledge the abuse. I was hoping that going longer between his sightings of me, the easier it would be for him to let go. Two years of my life I had given him. The abuse didn't start until a few months before I left. He would mainly shove me around, but he did slap me a few times. I stayed, though I'm not sure why. When he threw a punch and cracked my cheekbone, that's when I left. That's when I learned to fight back.

"No, it's not worth it." I shook my head. "He'll get the hint." I knew my father wouldn't do anything; he was just like him.

"This is bullshit, Gwyn, and you know it. He isn't going to stop, not until he kills you."

I laughed. "He isn't going to kill me. He wants to control me." I blew him off, but the gun in my bag said I knew he was right. "He just knows I'm the best he's ever had."

"Come on." He grabbed my bag, threw his arm across my shoulders, and guided us to the back of the bar where the guys were setting up their stuff.

"You ready for tonight? It's the big reveal," Alex Neilson, the drummer, asked.

I smiled the happy smile I knew they all expected. "As ready as I'll ever be, but we should get some good shots tonight. This place is great, and the lighting is fantastic. I still can't believe you landed a gig here." I was so proud of them. I could still remember sitting on stools in Jake's garage when we were kids. They were all older than me, my sister's friends, but they always let me tag along, so I was glad to help them.

I helped haul in some equipment and then sat behind the stage, getting my camera ready to shoot. The announcer introduced them, and the crowd started screaming in the packed area. My heart was full for them. For over an hour, I worked my way through the crowd, shooting photo after photo of excited faces, screaming fans, and the band as they played their hearts out. I got some really good shots.

At the break, I headed back to get ready. I didn't want to wear jeans, so I'd brought a skirt to put on with my cowboy boots. It was Boho-chic, and it suited me. I dressed for myself, and I dressed for comfort.

With my bag packed, I headed to the bathroom. I needed to get my fucking nerves under control.

∽

Jaycen

I stuffed some clothes in a bag then grabbed a few prints I'd purchased last year. They were the only real artwork I liked in the whole place. For some reason, they made me feel calm. One day, I wanted to go visit the places captured in the photos. There was a gallery downtown that had more; I just hadn't found the time to get back there and check them out.

At the hotel, I showered and threw on a pair of jeans and a t-shirt. After grabbing my jacket, I headed out to The Jewel. I really didn't want to go, but I'd promised Caden.

When we pulled up, the line was down the street. Chuckling to myself, I got out of the car at the door. I never waited in a line. Arrogant, yes, but these guys knew who I was. My eyes scanned the line. Maybe I could find someone to fuck. Being me, it wasn't hard, but nothing sparked my eye.

I nodded to the guy at the door, and he opened it for me. I grabbed a glass of bourbon and made my way into the crowd. The band was on stage, and they sounded good, but they were playing covers. A few times, I found myself walking into a woman with a camera in her hands. She stood almost to my shoulders but never picked her head up to look at me. She just apologized for running into me. It was annoying.

I decided to wait for their break and go have a talk with them, maybe see if they had any originals I could hear. Two bourbons later, they walked off the stage. After setting my drink down, I made my way to the back.

Walking up to the guys, I introduced myself, putting my hand out. "I'm Jay Ashford."

The lead singer put his hand out with a huge smile on his face. He knew who I was. "Mr. Ashford, I'm Kyle Long. So good to meet you."

"Listen, I'll admit that I'm not a fan of covers, but I like the way you guys sound. The way you play together is tight. Do you have any originals?"

"We do, actually. After the break, we have one coming up. We are only allowed to play one or two per venue. We're not big enough yet to play all our own stuff."

I had to laugh. It was the rule in most of these places. They hired these bands because they had a following, or the players were cute, or maybe people liked the way they played together. It sucked for agents and scouts. Reaching in my pocket, I pulled out my card and handed it to him. "Why don't you give me a call when you have some time? I'd like to hear them. I'm not making any promises, but I'd like to hear them."

I watched as he looked at my card. I swear to God, when he picked his head up, he had stars in his eyes. I think the kid had an orgasm right there.

"Come on, Kyle. We need to get back on stage," one of the guys yelled.

Kyle put his hand out. "Thank you, Mr. Ashford. I'll be in touch."

Chuckling, I turned and headed out. I could hear the band introducing someone. I was just to the door when perfection hit my ears and stopped me in my tracks. Turning, I could just see the woman's head above the crowd. I felt like I was being pulled by some invisible force back toward the stage. The woman standing at the microphone stunned me to silence. Her strawberry blonde hair framed her angelic face that was free of makeup. I stood there, shocked at the voice coming out of her mouth, out of her body. This woman had to be a professional singer. Why wasn't she the lead in this band? I needed to find out.

This song, the words, were pulling me in. The crowd stood still as I looked around. It was as if the room was transformed, and all the patrons had become mannequins. The only sounds were of the guitar softly strumming and her voice. I couldn't help but step forward, closer to her. My body was humming. Her eyes drifted closed as she hit the last note of the song. When she opened them, I was about a foot away from her, and she looked right at me. My heart stopped when she smiled, revealing the most perfect dimples. My God, she was stunning. Her eyes were so blue, reminding me of an evening sky overlooking the ocean.

With her voice no longer filling the space, the room grew so quiet you would have heard a pin drop. The crowd behind me erupted in applause, scaring the shit out of me. I jumped.

Her voice was soft, her "Thank you," almost inaudible. Then she disappeared off the side of the stage. I felt like a child. Everything seemed so out of control, my heart beating frantically in panic when she vanished.

I moved to the back of the stage to see if I could find her, but she was nowhere to be found. Did I imagine that? Surely, I didn't. I made my way to the bar. I needed a fucking drink. I stood there in shock, drinking my bourbon when I saw her in the mirror behind the bar, moving through the crowd. She was heading right toward me.

Casually, I turned in her direction, but she veered to the left and headed toward the bartender. I moved down the bar as he grabbed her up in his arms. "Oh my God, that was incredible," he said to her as he swung her around.

"Thanks. When everyone got quiet, I thought for sure they were going to heckle me off the stage."

Is he her boyfriend?

"You can sing here anytime you want."

She laughed. "Yeah, no thanks. Just practice for the big day. I'm going to head out. Take care, and thanks again."

Her eyes shifted and looked right into my soul. At least, that's how it felt. Her smile was small and short, and then she was moving again. I had to stop myself from following her. I just watched her walk out the door.

She mentioned a big day. *Was she getting married? Was this song for her future husband?* My eyes drifted to the stage. *Was one of them her fiancé?* I needed to get the hell out of here. *Why was I feeling so insane for this angelic woman?* She was just a girl in a bar.

CHAPTER THREE

GWYN

Oh my God. I nearly threw up. I had to get the hell off that stage, and who the hell was that guy standing there staring at me? My hands were still shaking. But on the upside, everyone seemed to like it. Quickly, I pulled on my jeans, then tugged off my skirt and stuffed it in my bag.

My head was spinning. Without thinking about it, I gathered up my gear and headed out. I needed to stop and see Tony before I left since he'd been kind enough to give them this gig. I never told them I gave Tony one of my prints for this opportunity. They didn't need to know that; they deserved to be here after all their years of hard work and playing in dive bars. This was definitely first-class for them. I think Kyle would kick my ass if he knew I was the money behind this Midwest tour. We'd been friends for so long, and giving my photos as payment was easy to do. I was still shocked that people wanted them and that they knew about me.

As I walked up to the bar, Tony came rushing over, grabbing me up in a hug. We talked for a few minutes, and when I turned to leave, the guy from the stage was standing there looking at me. I felt a weird pull to him. He was fucking stunning. Glancing at his watch on his wrist, I could tell he was rich; that watch cost as much as my Jeep. I smiled at him then looked away. He was too rich for my taste. Most of those men were major dickheads. Like my future brother-in-law was a total dickhead, but my sister loved him. Me? I believed they'd be divorced within two years.

Pulling myself away from the rich guy at the bar, I headed out the front door. My mind was still spinning from singing. My future brother-in-law didn't deserve this song, but my sister did. She was my big sister, and I loved her more than anything, so I'd smile and be the sweet little sister while I stood by her side and watched her make the biggest mistake of her life.

There were people all over the place outside—smoking, kissing, talking, and laughing— as I made my way through the parking lot. I just wanted to get the hell out of there and go home. I'd probably taken eight-hundred pictures, so I needed to sort through them and find the best ones. It was important that the band got good representation during this tour.

I pulled the fob out of my pocket and pushed it, unlocking my door. I was nearly there when someone grabbed my arm, spinning me around, and nearly made me fall on my ass.

"Who the fuck was that guy?"

It was fucking Gavin. I could smell the alcohol on his breath as he pulled me to his chest.

"Let me go." I pushed on him.

"Not in a million fucking years. You think you can just give this perfect fucking body to someone else? It belongs to me."

When he managed to grab my other arm, I tried to stay calm but told him sternly, "You're hurting me. Let me the fuck go." I tried to get away from him, but he kept his grip painfully tight.

"Who is he?"

"He's the fucking bartender. Gavin, please, just forget me. We are over."

He shoved me back against the Jeep, nearly knocking the wind out of me. "Like fucking hell, we are. Give me your keys and get in the fucking car, Gwyn."

"I'm not giving you shit." I made my move, trying to get around him, but he grabbed me from behind. Self-defense 101 kicked in. I bent over, flinging him to the ground on his back, and took off. He managed to grab my foot and tripped me, causing me to fall hard. I landed on my camera bag, slamming down on it with my ribs. My breath rushed out of my lungs, and pain seared through my ribcage.

I just closed my eyes and prayed he didn't kill me. Belligerently screaming at me and his violence growing, my thigh took the brunt of his kicks. But I couldn't scream because I had no air in my lungs. The darkness was coming. Fingers wove through and tightened in my hair right before my head was slammed down onto the unforgiving blacktop. Then there was blinding pain as I was ripped from the ground by my hair. He was pulling me up off the ground. I could feel each strand of my hair being ripped from my head as he released his grip, and I fell again, this time landing on my camera bag. The faint sounds of screams echoed around me, and the ground vibrating under me. There was a thud then, and it was over for me. Darkness took over, leaving nothing for my consciousness to grasp.

Jaycen

I finished my drink and walked out of the bar in a daze. Who was she, and why did I care? I felt strange. Never had I encountered someone like her. Her voice was that of a fucking angel. With my head down and my hands in my pockets, I left the bar and headed toward the parking lot. People were hurrying toward the side of the building, some of them yelling.

As I turned the corner, I picked my head up and watched some guy go flying through the air before landing on his back, which stopped me short. My eyes shot up as I watched her try to take off running, but the guy reached out and grabbed her foot, knocking her to the ground, where she landed hard with a thud I heard from across the lot. My mind wasn't comprehending what the fuck was happening, and I watched in horror as the guy got up and started kicking her.

"No!" I shouted, moving toward them. My eyes stayed glued on her, lying so lifelessly on the ground. He grabbed her by the hair and started slamming her head on the ground. When I got to him, he looked up just as my fist connected with his jaw, sending him flying into the Jeep behind her. His hands were full of her hair. He'd ripped it out when I hit him, and her body just fell to the ground.

He attempted to get up, so I hit him again and again. When I was sure he wasn't getting up, I spun around. People were surrounding her tiny, lifeless body. "Move!" I shouted, kneeling on the pavement next to her. Bending to touch her neck, I felt her pulse and let out the breath I'd unknowingly been holding. "Someone call the police." I didn't want to move her, so I laid on the ground next to her and took in her face. Blood was trickling from the gash on her head and down her cheek. The bastard had ripped her hair out. I couldn't see the other side of her face.

"Hey," I whispered. "Come on, beautiful. Open your eyes." I gingerly brushed my fingers along her cheek. God, she felt like heaven, so soft. "Hey."

She moaned. Her eyes fluttered. "Help me," she groaned. My heart broke right there.

"I've got you. He won't hurt you again."

"Help me up. I need to get out of here. Please."

I was confused by what she said. "Why? The police are coming, an ambulance."

"No. Please, help me. Take me away from here. I can't stay here."

I got up, totally confused by her words, by what she was asking me to do. I slowly pulled her up. "That's my Jeep. Please, get me out of here," she pleaded again.

I stood and lifted her in my arms. She weighed almost nothing. "Open the door," I said to some girl standing there. After sitting her in the seat, I pulled the seatbelt over her and then made my way around to the driver's side.

When I got in, I pushed the start button and took off, passing two squad cars and an ambulance on the way by. She passed out, so I headed back to the hotel. I pulled my phone out of my pocket and dialed Alex. The clock on her dash said it was eleven.

"Jay, what's up?"

"Listen, I need you to meet me at the Peninsula, the Lake Suite. No questions asked and bring supplies."

"Yep."

I couldn't get my hands to stop shaking. I knew I was driving way too fast, but I was terrified. I pulled into the garage, then ran around the car to get her out carrying her to the elevators. Thank God, this was just for my floor, so there was no chance of seeing anyone.

I carried her in and laid her on the bed in the spare bedroom, removing her bag and shoes. Her face was bloody, and she looked so small in the huge bed. There wasn't anything I could do but pace and wait for Alex. It felt like hours had gone by when the knock came. I ran out and ripped open the door.

"Jesus, Jay, what the hell is wrong?"

Without answering him, I grabbed his arm and dragged him into the bedroom. "Alex, man, she is hurt bad. She wouldn't let me take her to the hospital. Can you please make sure she isn't going to die?"

"Jesus fucking Christ, Jay, what the hell happened to her?"

"Some fucking asshole beat the shit out of her in the parking lot at The Jewel."

"Who is she?"

"I don't know. She asked me to help her, so I did."

"Get me some warm water and some towels so I can get this blood cleaned off her face."

Quickly, I gathered the supplies he'd asked for. I knew I should have taken her to the hospital. Standing there, watching him clean her face, it was pure anguish. She was so bruised. I wanted to kill the fucker who'd hurt her. When Alex lifted her shirt, I turned around. He's a doctor, and I'm a gentleman. "I'll be out here," I told him as I moved out of the room and closed the door.

I've never really been a pacer, but I was wearing a hole in the fucking carpet. My eyes shifted from the door to the clock on the wall. It had only been ten minutes, but those minutes dragged until they felt like hours. I needed a fucking drink. I should have called the police and let them know, but she'd begged me not to.

Picking up the bourbon, my hand shook. *Jesus, calm the fuck down.* The amber liquid burned as it slid down my throat, but my hands didn't stop shaking. I don't think I'd ever seen someone hurt a woman like that before. She was completely defenseless against him.

When the bedroom door opened, I nearly screamed like a girl, whirling around to see a look of confusion on Alex's face. "What?"

"Man, Jay, she was worked over."

"I know. I was there. I just wasn't fast enough. It happened so fast."

He shook his head. "She's pretty beaten up. Her face is bruised, but as far as I can tell, nothing seems to be broken."

"What about all the blood?"

"Her hair was ripped out. She's missing huge chunks, so her head is bleeding. Her ribs are bruised, but I don't think any are broken. When she wakes up, try to talk her into an x-ray."

I shook my head. "She didn't want to go to the hospital."

"Then bring her to my office, so I can check her out properly. I won't report it."

"That won't be necessary." We both turned around. She was leaning against the doorframe, holding her side. "I need to get out of here."

Alex moved toward her while I stood frozen in my spot. "Why don't you just rest for now? You're safe here. My name is Alexander Stevens, and I'm a doctor. Just get some rest and think about coming into my office. If you have broken ribs, it could compromise your lungs. You shouldn't be alone."

"I'm fine. It isn't the first time this has happened."

"Well, it will goddamn be the last," I nearly shouted.

Her eyes moved to lock with mine. "You're not the boss of me. I can take care of myself. He just got the upper hand."

It took everything I had not to shout. I was so pissed off still, and I knew that only a fraction of my anger was directed toward the asshole who'd hurt her. "He's done this to you before?"

She shook her head and slightly chuckled. "Don't pretend to be a

21

hero. I know men like you. He's a man like you—a rich, arrogant asshole. You think you can have or do whatever you want, not caring who you hurt in the process. I know. My sister is going to marry one of you. Me? Yeah, no, thanks." She stood there, staring at me and briefly glancing around at the room. "But I really don't want to drive right now. I have no idea where I'm even at, but I'm pretty sure, from the looks of this place, it's downtown, so I'll take you up on your offer."

Alex chuckled as he helped her back into the bedroom while I stood there totally mortified at the complete perfection of her thoughts. She had my number all right, and she didn't even know me.

When he came out of her room, he laughed at me. "Boy, did she just call you out on your shit."

Chuckling, I agreed, "Yeah, she did. Thanks, Alex. I'll try to get her to come by, at least for an x-ray."

"That would be good. Not a problem, my friend. Try to get some rest."

We walked to the door. "Don't think that is going to happen. But thanks, and please tell Alice I'm sorry."

Closing the door, I leaned against it, my heart slamming in my chest. *What the fuck is wrong with me?* I'd felt just like this when I found Ashley and that guy. I was so pissed that he was touching what was mine. But this girl wasn't mine. I didn't even know her fucking name. Looking around the foyer of this outrageous room, my eyes moved to the door of the room she was in. I should get her some ice. Yeah, ice.

Forcing myself to move, I found the wet bar and filled a towel with ice. I knocked on her door. "

Yeah?" she called out.

I opened it to find her in bed. Her clothes were on the bench, and the sheet covered her small body. Moving to the side where her face was bruised, I sat on the edge of the bed and gently placed the towel on her face. "I brought some ice; it should help with the swelling."

She was looking at me like I was crazy. Her finger pointed to my eye. "Seems you would know."

Chuckling, I reached up to touch the cut. "Yeah, I guess I would.

Well, I'll let you be." Standing, I forced myself to move. "Please, don't leave without letting me take you to see Alex. After that, you can forget you know me."

"I technically don't know you. But I won't leave. My side hurts like hell. I landed on my bag, and I would like to know if my ribs are cracked, so I'll let you take me."

I smiled and nodded. Jesus, I felt like I was fifteen. "My name is Jaycen, in case you were wondering." I kept moving to the door.

"I wasn't, but it's nice to meet you. I'm Gwyn. Thanks for the ice."

"If you need anything, just let me know. I'll leave my door open."

"This isn't your room?" She looked confused.

Smiling, I told her, "No, this is a two-bedroom suite. My room is on the other side of the living area."

She laughed. "Of course, it is."

It pissed me off that she thought I was an asshole because I had money. I mean, I actually was, but she didn't know that. I gave her one last look and closed the door. There was so much I wanted to ask her, but she didn't seem like she wanted to talk about anything with me. I grabbed a tumbler of bourbon and headed to my room.

Throwing back the contents, I texted Heidi and told her I wouldn't be in until later in the day. I stripped and dropped my clothes to the floor then crawled into the bed. My head hurt, and I needed to sleep.

Gwyn

Waking up in a strange place was different. Scary actually. I heard voices in the other room. When I walked out, I was stunned. The guy from the bar was there, as well as some other hunky man. What the fuck? I felt like I was in another dimension, the dimension of gorgeous men. One guy introduced himself as a doctor. I wanted to say something snarky, but I didn't. I was grateful the guy from the bar hadn't taken me to the hospital. That's all I needed.

I didn't want to be here, but fucking Gavin did a number on me. I was sure my father would be looking for me. I managed to go back in the bedroom, probably the bar guy's room. If I wasn't so beat up, I would sleep with him. He was fucking gorgeous, but after looking around and the fact that a doctor was here, let me know he was one of those rich, entitled assholes. Just like my sister's fiancé. But I need to be nice. I was grateful he'd saved me. At least, I hoped it was him who stopped Gavin.

Slowly, being careful of my bruised ribs, I undressed and climbed in the bed. The sheets felt like silk against my skin, but there was no way to get comfortable. I felt so dirty, but the doctor told me to wait a day to shower. Fucking bastard ripped my hair out. Reaching up, I felt the wet spots where chunks of hair were missing. I'd have to wear a scarf on my head until it grew back. *Fuck, the wedding is next week. How the hell am I going to explain this?* Maybe the hairstylist could style it well enough to cover up the bald patches.

Lying on my side hurt, and lying on my back hurt. Fucking asshole. There was a knock on the door, and I knew it was the bar guy. When he came in, he sat on the bed next to me and placed a towel full of ice on my face. It felt so cool against the bruise.

To be honest, I was a bit shocked when he told me this wasn't his room. But, of course, I let my attitude slip out. His name is Jaycen, and I nearly asked him to stay when he so gracefully walked out of the room, but I didn't. I wasn't in a place where I would enjoy a tumble in the sack with him. Not that I wanted to get involved with another rich bastard. But the guy was fucking gorgeous, so who would blame me?

As I lay there looking at the ceiling, my mind toiled over exactly what my father would say. I was pretty sure he knew by now that Gavin had either been arrested or was in the hospital. I hoped it was the latter, but I had no idea what happened. Looking at the door, I realized I should probably find out. Sleep wouldn't happen for a while because I was in too much pain.

Finding a robe in the bathroom, I slipped it on and quietly opened my door. The place was dark, but the moonlight shone through the huge windows, lighting up the space. It was very posh, very elegant.

Looking around, I saw a menu on the counter. "The Peninsula. Figures." I saw a door opened, so I headed that way. I needed to know what happened.

I stopped in my tracks just inside the doorway. "Fuck. Me." He was lying diagonally across the bed, his back to me, and he was buck ass fucking naked. Jesus, his body was sculpted. I swear his thighs were as big around as my waist. His broad shoulders were ripped with muscles even as he slept. My eyes moved down his back, my tongue licking my lips as my eyes landed on his ass. I felt myself tighten. He was perfect, absolutely fucking perfect.

My feet moved, bringing me to the edge of the bed. I looked down at his feet, which were huge. I swear to God, if I didn't leave now, I was going to crawl in this bed with him and fuck him. Shaking my head, I turned to leave but was caught short when my eyes fell on two of my photos. "What the fuck?" Did he know who I was? No one knew who I was.

"They're my favorite photos. I brought them from my apartment." His voice was soft.

I couldn't breathe. "I'm sorry, I don't mean to be in here." I heard clothes shuffling, then I felt the heat of his body as he walked up behind me, and my eyes closed. I swear if he'd touched me, I'd have fucked the man.

"What's wrong? Do you need something?"

I could feel his breath on my head. "What happened? How did I get here with you?"

"Come on, we can talk in the other room."

I shook my head. "I don't think I can move right now." My words came out as a whisper.

"Do you need help?"

It wasn't a chuckle so much as it felt like a whimper. "I was looking at you... naked... and I must admit that I'm a bit shaken by the sight of you."

"Should I be worried that I disgust you?" He was being a smartass.

"Disgusting is not a word I would use to describe what I was looking at. Please, just tell me what happened." I was getting dizzy with him standing so close to me. He smelled just as delicious as he looked.

"I'm not sure. When I walked out to the parking lot, I saw that guy flying through the air, and then I saw you fall to the ground and stop moving."

"I landed on my bag, and it knocked the wind out of me."

"I started running toward you, only I didn't know it was you when he got up and kicked you a few times. When he grabbed your hair and slammed your head on the ground, that's when I got there. I grabbed him, trying to get him away from you. His hands were wrapped around your hair." His fingers gently touched my hair; my breath froze in my lungs. "I hit him a few times, knocking him out. When I turned around, you were lying on the ground again. I laid down next to you until you woke up. You have an incredible voice."

I needed to get out of this room. Opening my eyes, I shifted them to the door, forcing my body to move. He gently put his hand on my shoulder. "Tell me why you didn't want to wait for an ambulance." His voice sounded kind and gentle, but I knew men like him. Gavin was a man like him. My sister's fiancé was a man like him. I wasn't sure I should tell him the reason why.

"I didn't want the hassle of dealing with the police."

"I don't believe you."

I moved away from him, away from his touch. "It doesn't matter. I don't matter."

As I moved to the door, I heard him chuckle. I turned to look at him. His head was down, but I could see the smile on his face. He lifted his head, looking me in the eyes. "There's where you're wrong."

"I don't want to matter. I just want…" Shaking my head, I walked out of the room. I made it to the door to my room when I heard him.

"Wait." I stopped. "I think you matter."

I couldn't stop the giggle. "You only think I matter because I'm pretty sure you want to fuck me."

"What makes you think that?"

I stepped forward into my room. "Because it's how I feel. Good night, Jaycen." I shut the door and took as deep a breath as my aching ribs would let me. This was crazy, like insanely crazy. What the hell was the attraction I felt for him? It had to be the fact that I hadn't had sex in months. Too complicated. I dropped the robe and climbed in the bed. I needed to sleep. I needed to not be here.

Jaycen

I stood outside her door for more than a few minutes. She wanted to fuck me. I think I forgot how to breathe. I sat in the chair in the living room, facing her door. Who was she? What was she talking about when she saw the photos in my room? Why didn't she want to deal with the police?

I had a million questions, but I knew I would never get any answers. I wanted them. I wanted to know who she was, why she believed she was nothing. She was so talented. That man must have been someone to her. He had to be her ex, her abusive ex. She was in an abusive relationship. "Holy shit."

I went to her door and knocked gently. I didn't hear her say anything, so I opened the door and walked in, sitting in the chair.

"He's your ex, isn't he?"

"It doesn't matter." Her voice was soft.

"Gwyn, did he hurt you while you were with him?"

"Only when he drank. This is old news; it's been old news for a while. He comes around once in a blue moon when he's drinking, and he tries to claim me."

"How often is a blue moon?" My voice was getting harder.

"Listen, Jaycen, this isn't really any of your business. You rescued me, brought me here, took me out of harm's way, and I've thanked you. That's all there is. Tomorrow, I'll let you take me to the doctor that I don't know just so I don't have to go see my regular doctor. I don't feel like being reported again. Usually, I just take care of myself, hide out until the bruises go away, and then I go away. I've been doing it for a while now. Please, after tomorrow, you won't have to worry about me or think about me ever again."

"That's no way to live." I couldn't believe what she was saying. "Don't you have a family to help you?"

She chuckled but not in a funny way. "He is my family's choice for me. My father thinks he walks on water. It's fucking sick how much my family loves him. I'm the one with the problem here, not him. He's just like you—rich, powerful, with good friends in the right places. Tonight's events will be blamed on you, for beating him up."

"What? No one should hurt a woman like that. I don't care how rich they are."

"Well, tell it to every fucking judge in this city. I'm the one with the problem. I'm the troubled one who provokes him. He is just defending himself. It's fine. Really, it is. I'm used to it. So, I just don't put myself at places he might be. I don't know who told him I was going to be there, but I can guess. It's over now. I have enough money to stay at a hotel if I have to."

"You'll stay here." I sounded demanding. Not sure I should have said that.

"I can't stay here."

"Why not?"

"I just can't."

"Then you can stay at my apartment."

She rolled over, wincing, and I moved to the bed. "Are you all right?"

"I'm fine. Why are you in a hotel if you have an apartment?"

"To make a long story short, a few months ago, I came home late and found my girlfriend fucking some guy in my bed. I haven't been able to sleep in it since. Kind of got drunk and shredded it. But I travel a great deal for work, and I wasn't there a lot. When I was, I would sleep in the guest bedroom. I don't want to live there anymore, so I'm going to sell it, but if you need a place to hide out until you heal, it's yours. This room is yours."

"Why would you do that? You don't know me."

I sat there looking at her swollen face, her bruises coming out in full force. I wanted to touch her. "Because it's the right thing to do. The place is just sitting there. Don't waste your money."

"I'll think about it. Thank you. Can I go to sleep now?"

When she rolled over, the sheet moved down her back. She was fucking naked underneath it. Jesus, her back had big bruises on it. My hand moved on its own, my fingers lightly touching the marks. "These are old."

She moved her arm around and pulled the sheet over them. "It's not your business. I'm a big girl and can take care of myself. Can I please go to sleep?"

I just sat there looking at her. What kind of person would do this to someone so tiny, so fragile? "Let me help you." I almost didn't hear myself say the words.

"I'm not worth the trouble. Trust me."

Standing, I moved to the other side of the bed and crawled in on top of the covers, lying on my side so I was facing her.

"What are you doing?"

"I'm not sure. Gwyn, no one should feel like that."

She smiled. "You feel like that. Or, at least, you did when you found her fucking someone else."

My lips quirked up in a half-smile, only because she was right. "Perhaps but let me do this. Come here." I stretched my arm out for her to snuggle to my side. I couldn't bear to think that she was so alone. She stared at me for a few minutes, and I could see her trying to decide what to do. Then she moved slowly to my side. When her hand rested on my chest, my heart nearly stopped before it started racing. She was so tiny compared to me, but she fit perfectly in the crook of my arm.

"You do know this is wrong, and we are probably going to end up having sex."

I chuckled. "I would never take advantage of a woman who was tattered and torn. I'm only here for support. Everyone needs to be held once in a while, with no expectations of anything else."

"Including you?"

"Including me." I wrapped my arm around her as her body came in full contact with mine. She was right. If she wasn't so beat up, I would have fucked her. Even bloody, she smelled like heaven. We lay there, barely breathing, trying to relax when she asked a question I couldn't answer.

"Why do men hit?" Her voice came out shaky and soft.

"I don't have an answer for you."

"Do you hit?"

"I have never hit a woman in my life. I don't think I've ever seen a man hit a woman until tonight. It was so infuriating and frightening; I was so scared for you. I thought he'd killed you. The fear was so real I could taste it. I can't even imagine how you felt."

After several minutes, she responded. "I think I was pissed that I fell on my bag and knocked the wind out of myself. I was prepared to kick his ass. I've been taking a self-defense class."

I smiled. "I think you should get your money back." I was being a smartass.

She giggled. "Yeah, me too."

I felt my hand move, pulling her closer to me. Her skin felt incredibly soft.

"Not all men hit."

"In my experience, they do. My father does, and my sister's fiancé does. I don't understand why she is marrying him. I tried to talk her out of it, but she says she loves him."

"Did you love him, the man who did this to you?" I wasn't sure I wanted to know the answer to that. She was silent for so long I thought she'd fallen asleep.

"I don't think so. How could I, when he would hurt me?"

She sounded groggy, so I didn't respond. I just laid still so she could sleep and feel safe. For some reason, I wanted to protect her, keep her safe, and I wanted to see her smile. Eventually, I fell asleep with her in my arms, where I could, at least for tonight, make her feel safe.

Gwyn

I nearly had a stroke when he got in bed with me. I wanted to fuck this guy more than anything at that moment. I needed to feel the release, to not feel anything but the euphoric release of an orgasm. He wanted to hold me, so I let him. I needed to feel something, some kind of kindness, and having the warmth of another human being that didn't want to choke the hell out of me felt nice. It was so easy to fall asleep in his arms. He was all muscle, and I wasn't sure he would feel comfortable, but he was too comfortable.

When I woke up, it was still dark out. I had no idea what time it was, but I needed to use the bathroom. He was so warm, and I was so comfortable. Rolling over wasn't as easy as it should have been; my side was killing me. The sheet pulled away from my body, and I still didn't register that I was naked, or that there was a strange man in the bed I'd just left. Sleeping naked was normal for me.

Jaycen

She woke me when she rolled over. I was going to get up and go to my room, but she got out of bed. I couldn't help but look at her, completely naked, not even wearing panties. Jesus fucking Christ, she was covered in bruises. Even her ass had bruises on it. My heart felt like it had a vice grip wrapped around it. I don't think I'd ever felt such overwhelming emotions before. It was so foreign to me. Was this empathy? Pity? Anger? When she turned on the light just before she closed the door, she turned slightly, and I got a perfect view of her fucking perfect tits. "Fuck." I didn't want her to feel embarrassed, so I grabbed the robe she'd left in the room and got up to stand by the door. I could hear her in there swearing; I would imagine it was because of her face.

The door opened, and I handed her the robe. She took it and slipped it over her shoulders. "Embarrassed, are you?" She was funny.

"No, not at all, just the opposite. I..." I didn't know what to say next.

"Don't worry about it. I just didn't think. Do you have anything to drink?"

"Yeah, come on." I walked out of the bedroom with her following me.

"That's some chest you have there," she muttered.

I realized I didn't have a shirt on. I didn't want her to feel uncomfortable. "Everything is here. I'll be right back." I pointed out the mini-kitchen and wet bar and went to grab a shirt.

As I walked into the room, she looked at me and smiled. "Do you have a t-shirt or something I can put on? Maybe some shorts?"

Nodding, I grabbed her a t-shirt and a pair of pajama bottoms. She wasn't shy; she just dropped her robe and put them on. I turned to give her some privacy, but I wanted to look at her. Hell, I wanted to pick her up and press her against the wall while I fucked her. But this wasn't the time.

She laughed. "Don't worry about it. I know you watched me walk to the bathroom."

"I'm a man, and you are a very beautiful woman. I'd be crazy not to look at you. But that was me just being a bastard. This is me being kind."

"Well, thank you, but I have nothing to hide."

"You're very forthcoming with your modesty." Hell, I didn't even know this woman, and she had no problem with getting naked in front of me.

"I suppose. Did you want anything to drink?" She was pouring herself some bourbon when I turned back around. My kind of girl.

"Sure, what you're having is fine."

She handed me the glass she'd just poured and grabbed another one. I went to sit in the chair. I felt like a gawking fifteen-year-old. I couldn't keep my eyes off her. My shirt came to her knees, and my pants swallowed her. She slowly moved to the couch and held up her glass in a toast, but didn't say anything. She just took a huge gulp.

"I know this is none of my business, but I can't help but wonder."

She looked at me. "You want to know why I was with someone like him. Why my family wouldn't do something to stop it. Why I didn't want to go to the hospital."

I nodded. "Well, yeah, that and about a million other things."

"It doesn't matter, Jaycen. After tomorrow, you won't ever see me again. So, what's the point?"

I didn't know what to say to that. I felt my body lean forward, and I set my glass on the table. "Gwyn, what would you say if I said that I would like to see you after tomorrow."

She chuckled. "You want to fuck me, that's all. I know because I feel the same way. I mean, who wouldn't want you? You're gorgeous."

She wasn't shy about anything. "I won't deny it. Yes, I would love to fuck you. I'd love to fuck you for days and days, but somehow, I don't think just once will be enough for me. But there is no way in hell I am going to touch you. What you have been through, what you are going through, doing that would only make me a monster, which I'm not. I am a bastard, but only because I'm hurt. The job I have makes me that way. But I think you might just need someone on your side. Someone who wants to be on your side. Someone who... well, someone..." Jesus, I was struggling. "Someone who might actually care about what happens to you." My voice was soft. I didn't want to freak her out.

She just sat there looking at me. The room was lit only by the moon outside. I could see her eyes glass over; she was fighting tears. "Why?" Her words were whispered.

"I'm not sure, but just think about it. Think about letting someone in. Like I said, I'm a bastard, yes, a rich, arrogant bastard. But I would never hurt you or let anyone else hurt you, not like that." I nodded toward her.

Her hand reached up to wipe the tear that fell silently against her cheek. "Thank you." Her voice sounded so small.

I couldn't stop myself. I moved to the couch, took her glass, and set it on the table. Pulling her into my arms, I settled her on my lap so I could hold her properly. "I can't even imagine how you must feel. How scared and alone you feel. I give you my word, Gwyn, that I won't ever hurt you like that. Let me help you in whatever way you need."

She nodded as she buried her head against my neck. "Yes." Her word sent chills down my spine.

CHAPTER FOUR

JAYCEN

I sat there in the dark with a very beautiful woman on my lap, and amazingly, I managed to keep my cock from making a complete ass out of me. She was in no shape to deal with me. I didn't think I had ever felt such compassion for another human being before.

She was so broken; her spirit was beaten out of her. But her defiance was strong. She was feisty and so vulnerable at the same time. I'm pretty sure, in all my thirty-five years on this planet, I had never met anyone like her. I certainly had never been in a situation like this.

As she lifted her head up, her fingers touched my face. "Thank you." Her words soft, sweet.

"Don't thank me, beautiful. Purely selfish reasons."

She smiled. "What would those be? Do you often save damsels in distress?"

"I've never saved anyone before. You are my first damsel. My reasons then were because it was the right thing to do."

"And now?"

"Now?" I chuckled; our faces were so close I could feel her breath on my cheek. Turning my head, I looked her straight in the eyes. "Now," I whispered, "I think I'd really like to fuck you someday."

"I think I'd like that."

"Yeah?"

She nodded, leaning her head forward. When her lips gently touched mine, I nearly lost my mind. I swear it short-circuited and fried every connection to the here and now. She pressed a bit harder, her tongue swiping along my upper lip. It took great resolve on my part not to ravish her. She tasted so sweet, with a hint of bourbon on her tongue. My lips parted a bit to gently capture her tongue. Fuck, she felt good. A small, sweet moan escaped her throat, and her hand spread across my cheek. Mine moved up to wrap around her neck. She was so fragile, but I wanted to really feel this kiss, to taste her whole mouth.

The slow, torturous movements of our tongues shot blood right to my cock. There was no stopping the blood flow; I was fucking hard instantly. I knew she felt it; how could she not since she was sitting right on me? I needed to stop, or things were going to get out of control.

But it wasn't me who pulled back. "I'm sorry," she whispered as she moved to get off my lap.

"Hey." She looked at me. "Don't do that. Don't apologize for taking what you want. What you need. I'm not that cold that I can't feel you shaking. I'm not that arrogant that I can't feel how scared you are."

She sat there on my thighs, looking at me. "Maybe being there tonight was supposed to happen."

"What do you mean?"

"You strike me as a man who doesn't do the bar scene, and I certainly don't do them. I was just there to sing a song."

I smiled at her, my hand moving the hair off her face. "I do, unfortunately, go to a great many bars. Part of the job description. Let me say this. That was a hell of a song. It pulled me back into the bar and right up to the stage." My thumb ran across her bottom lip. "You have an incredible voice." I moved my head closer to her. I wanted to kiss her again. Fuck, I wanted a hell of a lot more, but that was just my cock talking.

Her eyes fluttered closed as my thumb gently tugged on her lip. She didn't say a word as she leaned into me, touching her lips to mine.

Wrapping my hand around her neck, I laid her back on the couch and got comfortable next to her, being careful not to hurt her.

We kissed for a few minutes, then she snuggled into my side, and I wrapped myself around her. I'd never shared sweet kisses with someone before. It had always been frantic and sexual. Not this. This was sweet and sensual. Closing my eyes, I only hoped she would let me help her, let me keep her safe.

Gwyn

My mind raced a million miles a minute. I couldn't believe I fucking kissed him. Hell, I would have probably fucked him if I wasn't so goddamn sore. He seemed sincere, and I didn't really have anyone. Just my stupid sister, but her fiancé hit her. I don't know how many times I'd had to help her cover the bruises. But I felt safe wrapped in his arms.

The repercussions of what happened earlier were going to be a shitstorm I wanted no part of. I didn't want to go home because I just knew he'd be there waiting. At that moment, I was safe. I just needed my computer so I could work on the pictures. I'd worry about everything tomorrow. For the moment, I was safe.

When I woke, I could feel his cock on my thigh. He was awake. The room was full of light, revealing a new day. It amazed me how easy it was for me to let this man hold me; how easy it was to fall asleep.

"I'm sorry about this," he said softly.

I giggled. "I know it happens. Thank you for holding me."

His hand slowly moved up my back. "You hungry?"

I wanted to kiss him again, and he did say not to apologize for taking what I wanted. Tilting my head up, our mouths were so close. I moved that inch. His mouth opened to my advance, and time lost all meaning.

"Yes," I whispered between breaths, between our kisses. He smiled against my mouth. "You told me not to apologize for taking what I need. I think I needed that."

His laughter rang through the room. "Not one single problem with that. We should get you to Alex's to make sure you're all right."

It hurt getting off the couch, but I didn't want him to know how much. I wanted to take a shower, but that Alex guy told me not to wash my hair for a day or two. I didn't have any clean panties, and my jeans were trashed. Sitting on the bench, picking up my bag, I knew my skirt was still in there. I nearly cried as I slipped my hand into it. Pulling one of my cameras out, I found the lens was broken. "Fuck." That would be five hundred dollars to replace. I grabbed my skirt and pulled it out, and my other camera and lens came out in pieces. "Motherfucker." The fucking bastard had just cost me at least fifteen hundred dollars.

Closing my eyes, I put it all back in the bag. I needed to go home and see if my cameras were trashed as well. Fucking asshole. I should have just killed the bastard when I had the chance.

I dropped his clothes, put on my skirt, and stuffed my panties and jeans in my bag. I grabbed my bra and put it on. When I picked up my shirt, it was covered in blood. "Fuck." I stuffed it in my bag and headed out to the living room.

"Do you have a dress shirt I can borrow? My shirt has blood all over it."

He just stood there looking at me. I mean, my boobs weren't huge, but for my little frame, they were hefty. I watched him lick his lips as he turned around. "I do. Is white all right."

Giggling, I said, "Yes."

It was sweet how he came out of the bedroom with his head down and his arm sticking out with a white dress shirt in his hand. "Thank you." I took it and put it on. "Jesus. I could just wear this as a dress."

He lifted his head up. "I have a belt."

I picked my skirt up to show him my legs. "Probably not a good idea."

"Jesus, is that from last night?"

"This one here is, but no." I felt embarrassed, looking at his expression. "Listen, please don't feel sorry for me. Don't be kind to me because of this mess. If you are going to be nice to me, please let it be because I am me and you are you. I'm not sure I'll be able to deal with this between us if I think you are only doing it because I'm in this situation, or because I'm vulnerable because of it. I don't want anything to do with it if that's the case."

He shook his head. "No, don't do that. Don't demean yourself or be so cavalier about what happened to you, about what is happening to you. I am here in your corner, on your side because I want to be. No other reason. Okay?"

I wanted to believe him. Hell, who was I kidding? I needed to believe in someone. I'd been fighting with everyone for a year now. I just needed someone to be on my side, and what a shame it was that it was going to be a complete stranger. I nodded. "Okay."

"Good. Breakfast should be here any minute. I ordered everything. I know I didn't eat well last night. So, we'll eat and then we'll go. I already call Alex, so he is expecting us. We can take my car. If you want, I can have my driver take your car over to my apartment."

"You were serious?"

"Well, I know we don't know each other, so yes, I was serious. I'm not staying there."

"But you won't come and see me there. What if I want to see you?"

He was beautiful when he smiled a whole smile. "You can stay here with me. You have your own room."

"Can I think about it?"

"Of course."

Just then, there was a knock on the door. I had a great deal to think about. Should I stay in solitude, or should I stay with him? Either way, I needed to stay out of the line of fire. It was going to be bad enough when I turned on my phone.

Jaycen

When she walked out of that bedroom, I nearly stroked out. For years, I looked at Ashley with pride, with want, with desire. She was fucking gorgeous, her body perfectly symmetrical. But this woman standing in front of me left me speechless. In the light of the morning, in only her bra, even covered in giant bruises, she left me speechless.

Her small frame held an impressive chest. I saw them last night, but not like this, not cupped in a fantastic lace bra. What was it with men and lace-covered women? I swear, all the blood rushed from our brains and went right to our cocks. I could see her nipples, a deep rosy color, peaked and pushing against the lace. It was as if they were being strangled, and every fucking neuron in my brain was begging me to release them. But she was hurt, both mentally and physically.

When she asked for a shirt, I wanted to tell her no just so I could look at her. Walking into the bedroom was a difficult task. In the closet, I leaned against the wall. "Fuck." After grabbing a shirt, I took it to her. I couldn't look at her again, not that I didn't want to, but I wanted to fuck this woman. I could just imagine the burn when I pushed into her.

We took my car and driver to see Alex. I think I was still stunned by looking at her. My eyes kept drifting to her thigh. I wanted to touch her, but she was hurt and sore. I wanted her to stay with me so I could watch out for her. Who was I kidding? I wanted to kiss her, help her heal, and then fuck her. But somehow, I didn't think it was just going to be one fuck. I wanted her slow like her kisses—long, slow, and sweet.

We pulled up to Alex's office. "Is this guy expensive?"

I chuckled. "He's a friend, doing a favor for me. Don't worry about it."

She sat there looking at me. "I can pay. I just don't want to use my insurance card. It can be traced, and the fewer people involved in this, the less the repercussions will be for me."

What an odd thing to say. "What kind of danger are you in?"

She smiled. "Why? You thinking of backing out of your offer? It's fine." She opened the door to get out, but I put my hand on her arm.

"Wait a minute." She turned in her seat to face me. I watched her square her shoulders like she was ready to attack. "I told you I was in this with you, but it would be helpful to know what I am possibly up against. I do work out there in the world, and I would rather be prepared than not. Gwyn, someone is hurting you, repeatedly, and no one should do that to a woman."

She visibly relaxed. "I'm sorry. I'm just used to defending myself, the fighting, the shit storms for my rebellious acts. I'm sorry."

I nodded, and we went into Alex's office. Her x-rays didn't show any broken bones. Alex checked her head and then gave her some shampoo to wash her hair with. She had a small cut on her cheek that he put some butterfly bandages on. He gave us some for after her shower, and for my eye. All in all, she was just banged up.

In the car, I asked her, "Did you want to go see my apartment?" I didn't want her to stay there.

Her smile was tight, her dimples hollowed in her cheeks. "If you are sure, I think I'd like to stay with you for a few days, just until this soreness leaves. I don't think I could fight while being this sore."

My heart hurt for her. "You don't need to fight at all."

She nodded. "Do you think we could stop at my place and get some clothes? I need my computer as well."

"Is it safe?"

"Probably not, but I can't stay in hiding forever. I have things I have to do, and you're with me, so he won't hurt me again."

I nodded at her. She told my driver where to go. When we pulled onto her street, her body tensed. "Shit."

I looked out the windshield. There were two squad cars outside her building. "What's happening?"

"We can't stop. Please, keep driving. Can you head out of the city, please? I need to make a phone call."

"Gwyn, what's going on?" I was totally confused.

She didn't say anything for a long time. "Can you pull over here?" I watched her pull her phone out of her pocket. Turning, she looked at me. "I promise I will explain this all when we are alone," she whispered. "I need to make a call, and I just know that my phone will be traced when I turn it on."

"Turn the GPS off on it."

"What? There's GPS on my phone?"

I chuckled. "All phones have it. Here, give me your phone." She handed me her phone, and I turned it on. When it loaded, the missed calls and messages kept coming. I pulled down her settings menu and showed her. Turning it off, I handed her the phone. "Now, they'll have to ping the cell towers, and that takes longer. And they can only do it when you make a call or receive a call. You should be good."

She smiled at me, and it made my heart speed up. God, her dimples were so fucking sweet. "Be right back." I watched her get out of the car. She didn't close the door only moved away from it. "Daddy, what are you doing? Why are you staking out my apartment?" Pause. "He tried to kill me. That man was only defending me. No, Daddy, I'm not coming home. I'm twenty-seven years old. I have my own house. I am not coming home to live with you and Mom. I'm fine. Please, just stop this. He deserved what he got. I swear, I will disappear, and you will never see me again." She disconnected the call and shut off the phone. When she got in the car, she smiled a half-smile. "Can we please leave now?" She looked at me. "We need to get my car out of the hotel garage. It has a GPS tracker in it."

"Gary, when we get back to the hotel, could you move a Jeep for me and park it in the lot down on fifty-third?"

"Not a problem, sir."

I looked back at her. "There, problem solved." But I knew this wasn't the problem. It was much bigger. Who was this woman that she held so many secrets, secrets I wanted to know?

CHAPTER FIVE

GWYN

God, he was so mad. I was terrified to tell Jaycen who my father was, who Gavin was. He shouldn't have saved me. He should have just kept walking. I didn't know what I would do now. We got back to the hotel, and I gave my keys to his driver. I just want to be in some shape to defend myself.

I did the right thing by checking in with him; otherwise, he would have a fucking missing person BOLO out on me. I hated this life. I hated everything about it. I needed to get out of these clothes. I needed a shower.

When we walked into the room, he stood there looking at me. "I need to go into work for a little while. I'll stop at the front desk and let them know I have a guest for a few days. Whatever you need, just call downstairs, and they'll send it up for you. Okay?"

I nodded at him. "Thank you."

"When this is over, you can thank me. When I get back, we'll talk, all right?"

I nodded as he walked out the door. No one knew where I was, so I was safe for now. I walked over to the windows to look outside. My life wasn't worth the paper it was printed on.

In my room, I grabbed my bag and took out my lenses and cameras. I needed to document my body, but it didn't look like it was going to work. One lens had been completely snapped off, while the other was broken into pieces. But Jaycen said as long as I didn't make a call, my phone couldn't be traced. Looking at my phone, there was no way I was doing that, so I just crawled into bed and crashed.

Jaycen

Walking out of that hotel room was hard, but I needed to get to the office. I would figure out how to work from home for a few days. Maybe I'd play the sick card. My company was strong, but it was strong because I was a workaholic and made it that way. Ten years in the making. I started out slow in this business, and now, I was nearly a billionaire. Not that anyone ever wanted that as their goal. Well, arrogant assholes like me did. We wanted to own the world and everyone in it. My thoughts drifted back to Gwyn. Her fear of what was happening was very real, so real that it scared the shit out of me.

Sitting in my office, I planned for my number two to take over the day to day while I was out. He did it anyway if I was out of town. I packed my contracts in my spare briefcase and headed out. I wanted to be with her, to find out what the hell was going on. I stopped on the way back and grabbed a bag full of disposable phones so she could make her phone calls. I actually laughed when I thought about it. I felt like a criminal, a spy.

When I walked into the suite, it was quiet, very quiet. I didn't call out her name. Setting my briefcase down, I walked over to her room. There she was, sleeping in just my shirt. My eyes moved to the end of the bed where her bag was. As I moved closer, my eyes adjusted to the darkness in the room, and I could see what looked like cameras or pieces of cameras.

I toed off my shoes, wanting to hold her and kiss her again, which

I didn't understand because there was no way I was going to fuck this girl. Not yet, not until she healed, not until I knew the truth of what was happening. Why were the police staking out her apartment?

As I crawled onto the bed, she opened her eyes and smiled a small smile. What was it with this girl and her dimples? When she smiled, all conscious reasoning went right out of my head. "I thought you were going to work?" Her voice was soft and inviting. I laid down next to her, moving her hair off her face.

"I did. I went and picked up some contracts and gave a bunch of orders, and now, here I am. I'm going to work from here for a few days so we can hang out. I didn't want you to be alone."

She giggled. "I'm a full-grown woman. I'm used to being alone. It's not that bad."

I rolled onto my back, crossing my legs. "I know. I thought I would hate it, but I'm still so angry about what happened, and being alone seems to benefit everyone I know."

"Why?"

Turning my head, I laughed. "Because I'm a bastard to everyone. Yelling, bitching, you know us, throwing our temper tantrums."

She smiled a full-on smile. God, she was stunning. "Oh, I know the type. I'm sorry you had your life torn apart."

She was so sincere. "Thank you. When I get over this, I will probably be able to see the signs of her betrayal." I chuckled. "She showed up at my office yesterday, trying to convince me she was pregnant. She knows she screwed up. I would have given her the world, but she needed to fuck other men. I don't want a woman like that in my life."

"Yeah, I get it. The dickhead who did this was like that. He was my first, and apparently, I wasn't enough for him. That's when the hitting started, after I discovered him cheating on me."

"I had plenty of opportunities to cheat, but never once did I feel the need. She was all I ever wanted in a woman. Everything except a good heart. She doesn't have a good heart, and that hurts. But it's over now, and I just need to put this anger where it belongs and move forward."

"Do you think you'll ever love or trust like that again?"

"I'm not sure. I like to think I will. Last night, I thought about just going out and fucking someone, but I hate condoms, and until my test results come back, I have to use them. I'm not sure if she gave me something."

She giggled. "So, you were in the bar to pick up a girl, but instead, you got me."

Rolling onto my side, my thumb gently tugged on her bottom lip that was tucked between her teeth. "I literally picked up a girl."

"But you didn't fuck me." Her words came out in the sweetest whisper.

"No, I didn't. But I'm hopeful."

"You should stop touching me, Jaycen."

"I can't help it. You are so fucking beautiful. Angelic."

Her eyes closed as I continued to run my thumb along her lip, up her cheek. My fingers wrapped around her very small neck, and I leaned my head forward, our lips touching gently. When her tongue gently, faintly touched my lip, we got lost in each other. Jesus, this woman could kiss. Our bodies weren't touching anywhere except our mouths and my hand on her neck, and I felt like I was on fire.

I ended the kiss. "I'm not sorry."

"Me neither." Her eyes were dilated.

Just as slowly, I removed my hand and laid on my back. "I'm hungry. You hungry?"

"I am. I didn't want to order room service. I'm a bit leery of the fact that people might know I'm here."

"I didn't tell them your name, just that you would be my guest."

"Thank you. But yes, I could eat."

I got up and adjusted my cock in my jeans. "Well, then I'll go order us some food."

◞◟

Gwyn

I lay on the bed, watching him. He so casually adjusted his cock. I knew it was huge because I'd felt it on my thigh the night before. I felt myself get wet between my legs. My core ached, but shit, I wished it didn't. I couldn't bring this man into my mess. He was so beautiful. Closing my eyes, I could see him in my mind, lying on that bed last night buck naked. I'd struggled not to touch him.

I needed some clean panties. Some clothes. I needed to clean myself up, so I slowly got up from the bed. I couldn't walk around with my juices dripping down my leg. A small giggle escaped as I walked to the bathroom.

In the living room, I could hear him talking on the phone. "Yeah, I did. They were good. No, asshole, I didn't get laid. Listen, I saw Alex yesterday. He and Alice invited me out to their place this weekend for dinner. You want to come? That's fine. Yeah, I think I'm going to go. It's been a while since I've seen Alice. Okay, talk then."

When I came out of the bathroom, he was standing by the window looking out. "Everything all right?"

He turned. "Yep. That was just my friend. He's the reason I was in that bar last night. I just wanted to thank him. And no, I didn't tell him about you."

"Thank you."

"Hey, I bought you something today." He was moving toward the door.

"You did?" I felt giddy. He handed me a bag, and I looked inside to find it was full of phones. "What are these?"

"Disposable phones, so you can make calls and not have to worry about being found."

"What? Seriously?"

"Yeah, I saw it in a movie. I didn't know it was a real thing until I asked my secretary. So, I went and picked these up."

"Jesus, Jaycen, there are like ten of them in here."

"Twelve, actually. It's all they had."

Shaking my head, I went to sit on the couch. He came over and sat next to me as we pulled them out of the bag. I sat and watched him figure out how to use them, and then I excused myself to call my sister while he waited for the food.

"Hey, it's me."

"Gwyn, whose phone is this?"

"It doesn't matter. What is Dad doing?"

"Jesus, what the hell happened last night? Dad is so pissed off. He said you hired someone to beat up Gavin."

I laughed. "Of course, he did. Gavin tried to kill me last night, and some guy beat the shit out of him and rescued me. He ripped my hair out of my head. He was slamming my head against the concrete."

"He said you flipped him over your back when he tried to talk to you."

"Listen, I'm not going to fight with you, of all people, about this. You are just like Dad, justifying this shit. Like I deserved this, like you deserve it, and like Mom deserves it. Men aren't supposed to hit. I'm not going to let him hit me. It's wrong. He hurts me."

"So, where are you, Gwyn?" she snapped.

"I'm fine. I'll be there at your wedding just like I'm supposed to be. I was going to shoot the canyon, but now I can't. My face is black and blue, and I am missing huge chunks of my hair, so I am just going to stay where I am and heal."

"Who was the guy who beat up Gavin?" She was told to ask me these questions.

"How am I supposed to know that? I was unconscious on the ground with my head bashed in. Didn't someone identify him?"

"They said he picked you up and drove away in your Jeep. Daddy found your Jeep in a parking garage downtown. Gwyn, I'm scared for you. Is he holding you against your will?"

I couldn't help it; I busted out laughing. "Oh my God, you make me laugh. No one is holding me against my will. I honestly don't know who that guy was. I woke up in my Jeep and decided to walk away. I can't do this anymore. He nearly killed me. I almost died at his hands, all because I hugged the bartender at The Jewel. I'm not going to live like that. After your wedding, I'm leaving Chicago. Gavin Highland won't come near me again."

"Gwyn, I'm so scared for you. He is pissed. Daddy is pissed off at you." She lowered her voice, so I knew she was alone.

"It doesn't matter. I'll be at your wedding. You're my sister, and I love you, but I wish you weren't marrying him. He hurts you, and he isn't going to stop."

"He loves me." I could hear her tears.

"No, that's not love. It's not. Now, I have to go. I will call you next week. Don't worry about me. I'm safe."

"You really don't know who that guy was?"

"I really don't, why?"

"You should see Gavin." She chuckled. "Whoever it was that hit him gave him two black eyes, broke his nose, and knocked out one of his teeth. Then he was arrested. I was so scared for you."

"As I am for you. Please, reconsider this."

"I wish I was as strong as you are. Daddy will kill me if I cancel right now."

My heart jumped in my chest at the idea that she'd considered it. "You don't have to do this. Just remember that. You're not a slave."

I heard her struggle with the phone, and then his voice came through the phone.

"Why are you doing this, Gwyn? Come home so we can talk about this." Gavin sounded furious.

I didn't say a word. I disconnected the phone and turned it off. I was shaking and pissed, and I threw the phone across the room just as Jaycen walked in. He moved quickly, wrapping me in his arms. "Hey, what was that about?"

I wrapped my arms around his neck, pushing on his shoulders, and he gently picked me up. I wrapped my legs around him, and he sat down on the bed. His hand cupped my head to lay on his shoulder. I didn't mean to do it, but I burst into tears. It felt so good to have someone hold me, someone who was gentle with me.

"Aww, Angel, it'll be all right. I've got you," he whispered in my hair. I couldn't hold it in anymore. They were all against me. Even my own sister believed it was acceptable to hit and be hit. I shook my head as I sobbed in this man's neck. He didn't waver in his hold while I cried like a baby.

I couldn't tell you how long he held me, even after I stopped crying. Once I'd calmed down, I still didn't move. He felt so good, so warm, cocooning me in his embrace. He felt like salvation. Finally, I pulled back, wiping off my face. "I'm sorry," I managed to get out.

"Don't apologize. Never say you're sorry for feeling. You feel better now?" I nodded, looking at him. He was so fucking beautiful; my fingers touched his lips. "Angel, what are you doing?"

"You said," I whispered on his lips, "to take what," my lips touched his, my tongue touching his upper lip, "what I need." I pulled his top lip between mine. "I need this. I need to feel kindness, Jaycen."

"Yeah?" His breath puffed into my mouth as I opened it to take his.

I'd never moaned in my life while kissing a man before, but this man made me feel like making love with our tongues was erotic. He brought my body to life with just the touch of his tongue, his lips. He was so kind, so gentle with them. I felt him lay back, and his hands moved to my thighs. My chest pressed against him.

"Angel," he moaned out as his hands slowly moved to my ass, his fingertips resting on the outer part of my core. I knew he could feel my heat.

I didn't move, but our kiss continued. Nothing hurried, nothing rushed, just a sweet, gentle caressing of our tongues and lips. I slowed the kiss and sucked his top lip into mine before I raised my head, looking in his eyes. "Please," I moaned.

He gently shook his head. "Not like this. Not like this."

Then he stretched his fingers to touch the outer lips of my core. My eyes rolled in my head as I laid it down on his chest and could hear his heart pounding. He moved so slowly, like a snail as his fingertips gently moved along the space between my outer lips and my thigh. The caress was so hypnotic, so relaxing to me. My body calmed almost instantly. I was soaked from my desire, soaked from him, for him. His hands moved up my back, under the shirt I had on, around and up my sides, through the opening at the top by my face. Picking my head up, he kissed me again, slowly rolling us onto our sides. His arms tore open the shirt I had on as his hands still held my face, but it wasn't a rough move, rather a normal one to free his hands. He moved one hand down, wrapping it around my thigh. His hands were so big it nearly went all the way around. Our lips remained locked, still kissing. This man, this kiss, his tenderness calmed my soul. He was so very careful with me, so very tender. I had never been kissed like this man was kissing me; hell, I'd never been touched like this man was touching me.

He pulled back a bit, but I didn't want his lips to leave mine. "The food is here," he whispered.

I giggled. "I'm going to need a new shirt."

"I've got plenty. Thank you for the kiss." His eyes were so full of truth that it scared me. "You all right?" He let go of my thigh and moved the hair off my cheek.

"I'm better. Thank you for holding me."

"Anytime. Come on, let's go eat something, and then we can talk about this mess you seem to be in. We'll see if I can help you in some way."

Jaycen

I had to get out of that room. I wanted this woman in the worst way. But I knew how much of a dick move it would be to pursue that craving, and yes, it was a craving to have her. My body was drawn to hers, as if she was the air it needed to breathe. She was so sweet to touch. Bringing my fingers to my nose as I walked through the living room, I inhaled deeply. Fuck if she didn't smell like heaven with her sweet, musky scent. When I felt her heat, I nearly pushed my finger in to really feel how hot and wet she was. But those kisses, my God, they were enough to make a man crazy. I grabbed another shirt for her then made my way back into her room. She was sitting on the bed with her head down. *Fuck, I hope I didn't overstep.* I knelt on the floor in front of her, and she lifted her head to look at me.

"I know we don't know one another, but why won't you fuck me?"

I admit, she confused me. I had to chuckle because I didn't know how to tell her. "Angel." I put the shirt on the bed and pulled her onto my thighs.

"I'm sorry. It's just that you make me feel so beautiful, and sexy, and wanton."

"Don't apologize. You are beautiful and so very sexy." I took her hand, running her fingers along the bulge in my jeans. "I am very wanton of you, also." She smiled. "Come on, let's eat."

Later, we sat with me in the chair and Gwyn on the couch, looking at one another. I didn't want to push her, but I needed some information. "You want to tell me about the phone call?"

She shook her head and smiled. "It was my sister. She had a million questions for me, programmed questions. Apparently, you broke his nose, gave him two black eyes, and knocked a tooth out." She smiled. "Then he grabbed the phone from her, so I hung up and threw it across the room. My sister is afraid to leave her fiancé. She thinks our father will kill her if she cancels the wedding, but I don't want her to marry him. He's a monster."

"Tell me about your father." I tried to keep my voice level. "Tell me why she thinks he would kill her."

She chuckled. "Long story or short story?"

"Whatever story you want. I just need a bit of information, so I can figure out how to help you."

"Jaycen, short of marrying me, and I'm not even sure that would help, you can't help me."

He chuckled. "Why?"

"My mom's first husband, my sister's father, was killed by a drunk driver before she was born. Years later, she met my father, a policeman. When I was two, he was shot by some insane criminal."

"Jesus. Your poor mom."

"I know."

"But I heard you call him Daddy."

"My father now was my biological father's partner. He took up, I guess, where my father left off. My mom married him when I was four and my sister was six. He started hitting my mom a few years later. As we got older, he began beating on us. I don't know why my mom stayed. I mean, I can guess because she had two children. I never want children. I never want them to suffer the way we did. I had my tubes tied when I turned twenty-five. Now, my mom couldn't divorce him. I think he would kill her first."

"Do you really think he is capable of killing your mom?" What she was saying was terrifying.

"Oh, he wouldn't dare risk his reputation. Just like fucking Gavin; my father needs him, and he needs my father."

"Gavin?"

"The asshole you hit."

"Angel, I'm a bit confused."

"I know. I'm leaving a bunch out. I don't know how to tell you the rest. How to tell you who my father is, who Gavin is, without you wanting me to leave. I know you're going to throw me out, and I don't want you to." Her voice sounded almost childlike.

I didn't say anything. It was bad. It was going to be very bad. I wasn't so sure I wanted to hear this.

"Gavin is the Assistant District…"

I cut her off. "Attorney who is running for D.A.?" She nodded. "Who is your father?"

"Thomas James."

"The Commissioner of police?" She nodded.

I sat back in my chair, looking at her. Un-fucking-believable. She didn't move; she just sat there looking at the table like she was waiting for me to blow up. I stood and saw her flinch. When I moved toward her, she cringed, and my heart sank. Reaching for her, I gently pulled her off the couch and picked her up. She reluctantly wrapped her legs around me. I didn't say a word to her as I carried her into my bedroom. Climbing on the bed, I sat her on my thighs, taking her face in my hands.

"Don't do that. Don't be afraid of me. I will never hurt you like that. I may yell, but I would never hit you or any woman. Okay?"

She nodded. "I'm afraid that I've dragged you into this mess."

"You didn't drag me into anything."

"I asked you to help me, to take me away."

"What is happening to you, to your mom and your sister, is wrong. They are men with power, abusing that power. Nothing about that is right. Evil doesn't always win, you know."

"You can't possibly stop them. I've tried."

"Aww, Angel, we don't need to stop them, just expose them for what they are."

Her fingers touched my lips. "How?"

"I'm not sure. Angel, what are you doing?"

Her fingers pulled my bottom lip down, and her lips touched mine. "I like the way you kiss me. It makes me…"

She didn't finish her sentence. Instead, we got lost in one another. God, I could've kissed this woman all day.

We laid down and fell asleep for a little while. I woke when she got out of bed and walked out of my room. I didn't know where she was going or what she was doing, so I got up and followed her into her room. She was putting on her jeans. I nearly groaned out loud because she wasn't wearing any panties. My God even covered in bruises she was stunning. My cock hardened in my jeans.

"What are you doing?"

"I can't stay here. I can't let you get involved in this."

"What? What happened?"

"You make me feel alive, like nothing I've ever known. It's suicide for you to help me, and I can't let that happen to you."

I moved across the room and pulled her close to me. "It's not your decision; it's mine. What brought this on?"

"The way you kiss me. I'm getting attached to the way your lips feel on mine, and I can't get attached to you. I have to fight to save my own life, and I can't ask you to do it for me or with me."

My heart fluttered when she said she was getting attached to me. "Then I won't kiss you anymore. Where are you going to go?"

"Home, just like I always do."

"Jesus, Gwyn, don't let him hurt you again. I don't think I can handle knowing you are out there alone."

She pulled away from me. "I'm not alone. I bought a gun, and if I have to use it, I will."

"No. No, Gwyn. Just stay here. I'll keep my hands off you. Please." My head was spinning. The fear I felt was very real. How the hell did I get so attached to her in just a day? This was crazy. I had to let her go. I couldn't make her stay against her will.

"It's not your hands; it's mine. Don't you understand? I have never been this attracted to someone in my whole life. I don't even know you, and I'm so willing to give myself to you. What the hell is that? I kept my virginity until I was twenty-five years old, and now I'm some kind of wanton slut. This isn't going to end well."

I couldn't help but smile.

"What? What's so damn funny?"

"Nothing. If you are going to leave, then take the phones with you. I'll give you my cell number, so if you need me, or need anything, promise me you will call."

She stood there looking at me like I'd just cut her head off. "Seriously? You are going to let me go, just like that?"

I grabbed her bag off her shoulder, putting it on the bench, and then I bent down to pick her up. I climbed onto the bed, laid her on her back, and leaned over her tiny frame. "I don't want you to go. I don't think I ever want you to go. I want you to stay with me. Stay with me until we can figure out what to do, how to help you. Stay with me for the rest of your life. Don't go. I can't force you to stay here. I can only hope that you won't go. If you leave, I'm sure I won't sleep. I will do nothing but worry about you. Don't go, Angel. Don't go."

Her eyes filled with tears, and she reached her hand up to touch my face. "I'm terrified of how I'm feeling. I've never felt this way from just a kiss."

"I'm coming off a heart-breaking break-up, and trust me, I have never felt a kiss like the ones you give me." My voice was low and deep from the desire filling my veins. Slowly leaning down, I put my lips close to hers. "Angel stay with me," I whispered on her lips as I kissed her.

When she put her hands on my face, it was over. I wanted this woman. I wanted her to stay with me always. I stayed suspended above her, taking my time and enjoying her mouth.

Pulling my head up, my eyes opened slowly to see the tears sliding down the side of her face. "You sure?"

"I've never been surer of anything in my whole life."

"I don't want to leave, Jaycen. I want to stay here with you. I feel safe here. I feel desired, wanted."

"You are all those things and more. Now, get these clothes off and relax." She smiled a full smile, her dimples showing deep in her cheeks. *God, could this woman be any more beautiful?*

"I need some new panties and maybe some clothes."

"Well, then we should go shopping." I pushed up on my knees, trapping her legs between mine.

"If I use my credit card, they will find me. I would need to go to the bank and get cash. Can we do that?"

"I'll do you one better. How about I go shopping for you? Just tell me your size, and I'll go." I didn't mind buying her some sexy panties.

She started giggling. "You would go buy me panties and bras?"

I wrapped my hands around her thighs. "I've bought my fair share of panties."

"Fine, I'll let you, just so I can see what kind of taste you have." She sat up, pulling her legs from mine. She got up on her knees and took off the shirt she had on. I watched as she reached behind her and unhooked her bra. The bruises were nearly black on her body, but they disappeared from my sight when she slid her bra off.

"Jesus," I moaned.

Her smile didn't fade as she looked at the size tag. "I wear a 32C. My panties are a double zero. My jeans are size zero, and I wear a small in shirts. Think you can remember that?"

I was stupid, completely and utterly stupid, looking at her. Hell, I thought Ashley was perfect, but she didn't even come close to Gwyn. "You are fucking perfect," I moaned. Her nipples were hard and pointing up a little, beckoning me, causing my mouth to water. Her tits were perfectly symmetrical. I could feel my hand twitch. I wanted to touch her, to gently fill my hands with perfection.

I saw her head move down to her chest then back to my face. "You've seen boobs before, right?"

Licking my lips, I told her, "More than my fair share, I'm sure."

"Then why do you look like a child standing in front of a candy store window?" Her hand reached up to touch my face, drawing my eyes to hers. "Do you want to touch me, Jaycen?" she whispered.

My hand moved to her waist and then around her back, my fingers wrapping around the other side. "With all that I am, yes, Angel, I want to touch you." I pulled her closer to me.

"Do you want to fuck me, Jaycen?" Her fingers moved to pull my shirt up. "I want you to fuck me. I want you to touch me. If I stay with you, will you eventually have your way with me?"

I smiled because, how could I not? "Are you teasing me, Angel?"

She managed to get my shirt to my neck and then leaned her chest against mine. "Yes."

I lost my shit, and my mouth crashed down on hers. It wasn't sweet and simple. It was possessive and savage. This woman was going to cause me to lose my resolve, but I couldn't. She was hurt, and I didn't have any condoms. But fuck if she didn't feel like heaven against my skin. I took her fire, her passion in our kiss. Pulling back, I looked at her flushed face. "I won't fuck you, make love to you, or anything else except this," I kissed her, "until you are healed, and my test results come back. I hate condoms, and I want to feel your silken walls as I slowly push deep inside this incredible body of yours and claim you, make you mine. Is that acceptable to you?"

"You want to make me yours?" I felt her tense up.

"I don't think I want anyone else to have you, to taste you, to kiss you, to feel you. I think I would like to be the only one."

"Yeah?"

"As weird as this is, yeah. Now, can I go calm the fuck down, so I can go get you some new clothes and heaven forbid some new panties."

She giggled. "Go." Lying back on the bed, she undid her jeans. "I'm taking them off, so if you don't want to be tempted anymore, then you should leave because I'm going to take a nap while you are gone, and I sleep nude." I sat there frozen as she unzipped her jeans and pushed them down to her thighs.

I moved back and pulled them the rest of the way off. She rolled onto her side and snuggled the pillow. She was fucking perfect—the curve of her hip, the size of her thighs, the place where her legs connected to her ass. My hand moved on its own, and my thumb pressed into her hip bone as I pressed my fingers into her ass. Her eyes stayed glued to mine. "Go, Jaycen, so you can get back." I smiled and bent down, planting a sweet kiss on the outside of her ass. I had to get the hell out of her room, off her bed. I wanted to taste her, to hear her scream when I made her come. I forced myself to get off the bed and walk out of the room.

Grabbing my phone, I took my hard as fuck cock and left. I was on a mission.

Gwyn

I had no idea what I was doing or why. I didn't even know the man, but I wanted him. So much so that I was constantly wet between my legs. I mean, Jesus, I'd never dripped before. The inside of my thighs could've been a fucking slip and slide. But what was coming, the shit storm that was ahead of me, ahead of him, was going to be tremendous. My father wanted Gavin as the D.A. I knew he was a bad cop, a crooked cop, and I had the photos to prove it, but how the hell could I take down my father? Who the hell would I even go to?

When he grabbed me and laid me on this bed, I thought for sure he was going to fuck me. But he didn't; he wouldn't, and I needed to respect that. I couldn't help smiling, knowing he was out there buying me panties. I was more than excited to see what he came back with. What excited me the most was knowing he would take them off me, one day.

I closed my eyes. I wanted him to be here with me, and I didn't know why. I didn't even know his last name or what he did for a living. Well, he didn't know that about me either. He didn't know that I was the photographer who took those prints he has displayed in his bedroom. Maybe that was why he was waiting to fuck me. I thought he really might be a good guy, one of the good guys that didn't hit.

Finally, my body relaxed, knowing I was safe, and I slept.

CHAPTER SIX

JAYCEN

Jesus Christ. Standing in the elevator, my heart was racing and my cock hard as steel. I had no idea what I was doing. I'd just begged the woman to stay with me. For some reason, I wanted to save her. *Is this like damsel in distress syndrome? I saved her, so now I have to have her?*

The elevator doors opened, and I was off on my mission with a smile on my face and a bounce in my step. I grabbed a cab and headed off to a wonderful place I knew. It was fun buying her things—sexy little panties, silk pajama bottoms to wear around the hotel room, and some sexy camisoles. I bought her a few pairs of jeans and some tops. I knew she liked different types of patterns from her skirt. All in all, I spent three thousand dollars, and when I returned, I had more than a few bags.

When I got to the hotel, my phone buzzed in my pocket. Setting the bags down, I pulled my phone out of my pocket, swiping it on. "Jaycen Ashford."

"Jay, it's Alex. I got your test results back. You're clean, and your sperm count is the same. No swimmers."

"Thanks, that's good news."

"How's our girl?"

"She's doing better. Alex, I'm worried about those bruises. I've never seen anything like them. You sure she's all right?"

"Yeah, they're just surface trauma. They're bad, no doubt about it, but she should recover with no problem."

"Thanks. Listen, if anyone asks you, you never saw her, and you don't know anything."

"Is she in trouble?"

"Yeah, but not the kind you're thinking. Her ex is very abusive. That's who was beating the shit out of her when I found her. He's a real winner."

"Man, why do men do that shit? I would punch a hole in the wall before I ever raised my hand to Alice. I mean, people get in heated arguments, but to hit a woman, that's scum of the earth low."

"I totally agree with you. Hey, thanks again. We'll talk soon. I'm getting in an elevator right now."

"Okay, talk soon."

When I walked out of the elevator, my phone buzzed again. I didn't look, just swiped it on. "Jaycen Ashford."

"Jay, please don't hang up on me. Where are you? I've been by the apartment and the office. Heidi said you haven't been in."

I swiped the card and walked into the room while she was talking, then set the bags down. "Ashley, I told you to forget you know me."

"Jay, how can you say that? I love you."

"I'm not doing this with you. Just forget my number." I disconnected the call and then blocked her number. The rage was building again; she'd fucked me over good. I couldn't see straight. My eyes zeroed in on the bottle of bourbon across the room, and my feet were moving. I was halfway there when movement across the room caught my attention. When I turned my head to see her standing there wrapped in a towel with her hair soaked, everything came full circle. I didn't have time for this rage toward someone who didn't matter anymore. Looking at her, it hit me that my problem with Ashley was nothing compared to what this woman standing across the room had been through. I realized that I was acting like a spoiled rich bastard who didn't get his way. Looking at her, I felt myself calming down. I knew at that moment that what Ashley did to me didn't matter anymore.

"You're a sight for sore eyes." I smiled at her, and it didn't feel forced.

She slinked toward me. "Why are your eyes sore, Jaycen?"

I smiled. "They're not, Angel. Just angry." All the anger just washed away.

"What happened?" Her voice cracked.

"Oh, my ex just called, crying, wanting to know why I haven't been to the apartment or to work. She told me she loved me; you know, same shit different day."

"What, nothing about the baby?"

I laughed. This was what she did with her smart mouth and her lack of fear of saying what was on her mind. "No, nothing about the baby."

"I'm sorry that she has you so upset."

I moved toward her, my hand touching her face. "You don't need to be sorry. It's done. It's been done for a few months now."

"What is it about exes? Why can't they just deal with what they did and move on?"

"I don't know. I suppose they realize what they've lost and are desperate to get it back."

"See..." She turned and walked over to the bourbon, pouring two glasses. My kind of girl. "What I don't get is why, if they knew what they had, would they destroy it in the first place?"

She handed me a glass. I will admit I was very distracted by the fact that she was in a towel. "Thank you. I bought you some things." I took a drink then handed her my glass. I went to the door to get the packages. "Come sit on the couch so I can show you."

She laughed as she sat down. "So, you're going to show me panties and bras that you bought a complete stranger?"

I laughed. "A complete stranger whom I've seen naked more than once, so I think you might not be a stranger anymore. Not to mention, you've seen me naked."

"Just your back and ass, so that doesn't count. Oh, and those giant feet of yours."

I reached into a bag. "You know what they say about men's feet, right?"

She busted out laughing. "I think it's the hands. Big hands, big cock. Little hands, little cock."

I looked at my hand. "What would you say, big or little?"

"Well," she took my hand in hers, "I would say average." She giggled. Damn, her dimples were amazing.

I pulled my hand away. "Anything but average." I looked in the bags and found the one I wanted to keep from her. "Here you go." She looked at me then at the bag that I'd set aside.

"What's in that one?" She nodded at it.

"Something I bought you for later."

"Later?"

I leaned in when I saw her eyes dancing and whispered, "For when I fuck you."

She swallowed hard. "So, you are going to fuck me?"

"One day, I hope, but I need to be sure that I will be the last and only man you ever fuck."

Her giggle rang through the room. "You think?" She turned her head to look in the bags.

"Oh, I know," I replied. She pulled out a bra and panties.

"Why would you spend two hundred and fifty dollars on a bra and panty set? This is crazy, Jaycen. I thought you would go to a regular store, not some fancy place like this. This is too much. I can't accept these."

"Don't be ridiculous. You deserve to have fancy things. These are beautiful, and I think they will look amazing on you."

"Yes, they are beautiful, but it's too much, too expensive."

"Well, then you probably shouldn't look in the other bags." I smiled at her and picked up the bags.

"Oh, no, you don't." Reaching for them, her towel came undone, and all movement stopped on my part.

"God, Angel, even covered in bruises, you take my breath away."

"Good, now give me the bags."

I laughed, handing them to her. She took them and the bag with the bras and panties and stood, her towel falling to the couch, and just walked away to her room. My eyes stayed on her the whole way. She had a perfect ass, the light showing through the gap between her thighs. I couldn't wait for the bruises to go away so I could watch her skin pink up as I bit her. My cock hardened. Man, I needed to fucking release.

~

Gwyn

I left my towel on the couch. I had no idea what the hell I was doing or why I felt the need to walk around naked in front of this man. I never did things this, like ever. But fuck if he wasn't the fucking sexiest man I'd ever seen.

With a stupid smile on my face, I started going through the bags. "Oh my God." He bought me ten sets of bras and panties. God, they were so beautiful. Different kinds of panties.

"I thought they would all look good on that incredible ass of yours."

I turned to see him leaning against the door frame like sin on a stick. My smile was huge. "Well, thank you. I guess this means you are going to want to see what they look like."

He smiled and moved toward me. "I'm particularly enjoying exactly what you are wearing now." I didn't get a word out of my mouth before he picked me up and walked to the wall, pressing me against it. Our faces were only inches apart. "You are so fucking beautiful; it should be a crime that you have to cover this body up." I swallowed. What the hell could I say to a man who said that? His lips brushed mine in a sensual tease as his hands wrapped around my thighs. "Will you let me have you, Angel? When your body is healed, will you let me have you?" I could taste the heat of his breath on my lips. Bourbon.

64

"Yes. Please, yes."

His tongue licked my lip. "All of you?"

"Yes," I puffed out. I was so fucking horny, so wet. My core felt tight with anticipation. "Please," I moaned. His fingers were right there at my opening. He was teasing me, and I fucking loved it.

His hands slowly let go of my legs, his cock pressing into my stomach as he moved them up my sides. I felt his thumbs barely brush the outside of my nipples as he moved them up to wrap around my neck and hold my face before he devoured my mouth in his slow, sweet, tortuous kisses. I swear to God, I came like a fucking freight train. A low moan escaped my throat. My core was pressed against him as my back arched off the wall. Every fucking muscle in my body strained. The pain in my side was tremendous from the pressure.

I felt his hand leave my face and move down my body. His fingertips gently touched my core as he wrapped his hand around my thigh. "Oh, Angel, look at you," he whispered. "So beautiful." His mouth covered mine, just as his fingertip brushed across my clit, sending my body spiraling into an orgasm like I'd never known.

"Ahh," I cried out, my head falling backwards against the wall as my body shook. He stood there, holding me, watching me. When he pulled back, I knew he was looking at my tits. I could feel my nipples tighten so much that they hurt. My breath came in short gasps as I calmed down. Licking my lips, I raised my head up to see him looking at my face. I didn't know what to say or what to do. My fingers touched his lips. "What was that?" My voice didn't sound like my own. I almost giggled; I felt like I'd been transformed into something else, someone else. His eyes closed, and he slightly shook his head as I touched his face. His hands gripped tighter on my thighs as his mouth sat slightly open. "Who are you?" I whispered on his lips as I kissed him. He turned us and moved to the bed, laying me down. I watched his eyes as he pushed up on his hands to look at me. Without a word, he pushed off the bed and walked out of the room. I laid there as my body hummed with a silly smile on my face. Looking at the door, I couldn't help but wonder what was going on in his head. I got up and put on some of the clothes he'd bought me.

Jaycen

I needed to get out of that room and away from her. I wanted her so bad, my hands shook. I'd never seen a woman orgasm like that. I felt her whole-body shatter. It took all my resolve to walk away. I had to walk away; I needed to walk away. I'd been about to fuck her, and I didn't want to do that yet.

Just the thought that another man touched her like that, then hurt her like that, made my blood boil. I didn't want her to suffer, to feel pain; she didn't deserve that. I needed to not be here right now. I needed to talk to someone, but I couldn't let anyone know she was with me, or discover my part in rescuing her, not yet. Not until we figured everything out.

As I paced in the living room, she appeared in the doorway, wearing a pair of the silk pants I'd bought her and a t-shirt. "These are so beautiful. Thank you." I smiled at her. "Are you all right? You kind of checked out in there."

I wasn't sure I could explain what I was feeling or why I felt so possessive of her. She moved closer to me, and I took a step back. The confusion in her eyes cut me like a knife. The way her forehead crinkled as she questioned me with her eyes felt like a hot poker searing across my skin. "I've never felt that before. That bastard hurt you, touched you, did horrible things to you, and I'm struggling with that fact."

She shook her head and smiled sweetly. Damn those fucking dimples, they would be the end of me. "No, he never did that to me. He never took the time; he never took care."

"How is any of this possible? I was in that bar doing a favor for a friend of mine, and now I'm here with you, experiencing probably the most fucking erotic moments of my adult life. I have never felt a woman come like you just did. I walked out of there because I wanted to do it again and again. I want to..." I couldn't say it. I couldn't make her feel less than what she was.

Her smile didn't waver. "I've never come like that before." Her voice was soft. "Jaycen, I don't know what is going on or what is happening here between us. We are complete strangers. I don't even know your last name." She laughed. "You just gave me the best orgasm I've ever had, and I don't even know your last name."

"Ashford." It was all I could say.

"James." She smiled.

We stood in the space just looking at one another for the longest time. She was the one who finally spoke. "I need my computer. I have to go home to get it. Will you come with me?"

"Is that a wise choice?"

"Probably not, but you have a life, and I have one, and mine, well, I need my computer to do it. If we are trying to keep you out of this, then you probably shouldn't go with me."

"I can't let you go alone."

"Unless you know someone who has no connection to you that will go with me, then I'm going alone." She wasn't being mean or shitty; she was just so very matter of fact about it. I watched as she turned and went back into the bedroom. A few minutes later, she walked out in her bloody jeans and her boots. She'd put makeup on her face, and I could hardly see the bruises. "I'll take a cab."

I walked over to the desk and wrote down my address. "Have the cab take you here when you leave your place. Go in, and I'll have my driver waiting for you inside. He can take you down to the garage and bring you back here." She gave me a funny look. "In case you're being followed."

"He won't hurt me again, not with the police there. He's afraid of my father, and if he thinks my father saw my face, he won't hurt me again. This is extreme, even for him. The bruises are always in places that can be hidden with clothes. Even my sister's fiancé and my father know to never hit in the face. I promise I'll be back."

"Take one of the phones and call me if he shows up."

She picked up one of the phones. "What's your number?" I told her and then heard my phone vibrating on the counter after she dialed it. "I'll be back in less than an hour."

As she walked out the door, every molecule in my body knew it was wrong to let her go. I didn't fucking care who was involved; I couldn't let her go alone. I grabbed my phone, jacket, and room key and bolted out the door. She was standing at the elevator when I trotted up next to her. "I can't let you do this alone."

She laughed, putting her arm through mine. "Thank you. I was a bit worried you didn't care."

"Oh, I care, Angel. I care."

Gwyn

When I walked out the door, my heart sank. I was sure he didn't care one way or another if I came back. I was sure he just wanted to fuck me, and I was okay with that; hell, who wouldn't be? But I wanted us to be something more. It was crazy to think that might be possible since I'd known him for less than forty-eight hours. How could he care about me in such a short time? When he walked up next to me at the elevator, everything changed for me. I hoped for him, as well. He wasn't afraid of what lay ahead of us, because if he was, he wouldn't have been standing next to me.

"Let's take a cab," he said.

"I don't have any cash. We need to stop at the bank anyway. I have something there that I need, something I think you should look at."

"The bank it is."

"We can walk from there; my house is only a few blocks over."

"You put makeup on your face." He hailed us a cab.

I climbed in, and he slid in behind me. "I did. I was going to the bank anyway, and I figured it was probably a good idea to cover what I could. Now, you're with me, which I was really hoping you would be, and I didn't want people to think you did this."

"Sweetheart, anyone who knows me knows I would never do anything of the sort."

I just smiled and told the cab driver where to go. At the bank, I went to my safety deposit box and got my external hard drive. Before we left, I gave it to Jaycen. "Hide this someplace on your body, just in case." I watched as he slipped it in an inside pocket of his jacket. As we walked down my street, I could see there weren't any squad cars staking the place out, but that didn't mean they weren't there. It didn't take long to grab my computer and my other camera bag. We were in and out in a matter of minutes, then walked a couple of blocks away before hailing another cab. Just as Jaycen stuck his hand out, a man in a suit walked up to me. "Miss James?"

I looked at him and shook my head. "I'm sorry, you have me confused with someone else."

Jaycen had turned and put his hand on my lower back. "Is there a problem?" he asked the guy.

"Are you Gwyn James?"

"No, she told you she isn't. This is my wife."

"And you are?" He looked hard at Jaycen.

"None of your fucking business." He turned me away and opened the cab door, gently pushing me in and climbing in next to me, and we left the man standing on the sidewalk looking very confused and upset. "What was that?"

"I'm not sure, but I can guess." My father, no doubt, was trying to scare me into going home. The guy had probably planned to grab me and take me downtown to my dad's office. "I'm glad you came with me. Thank you."

"Gwyn, who was that?"

"One of my father's goons. I'm sure he was going to take me to his office, so he and Gavin could convince me to go home. He's done it before." We didn't talk on the ride back to the hotel. When we got into the room, I went and took off my jeans and put back on the pretty clothes he'd bought me. Then, after washing the makeup off my face, I grabbed my camera and made sure the memory card was in it before walking into the living room. "I need you to take pictures of my face, head, and leg."

He sat there looking at me. "Why?"

"I'll show you when we are done. Would you do this for me? I don't have a tripod with me; otherwise, I would do it myself, but I can't see my head."

He stood and walked over to me. With his finger under my chin, he lifted my head. "I will do whatever you want."

I smiled. "No, you won't because I'm pretty sure I want to sleep with you, and you won't."

He laughed. "Oh, but I will. I want to see your skin pink up when I sink my teeth into you, and I can't do that until you are healed. Now, show me how to work this camera."

I showed him, and he took about twenty pictures of me. Lying on the bed with my laptop and all my memory cards, along with the external hard drive, I got to work. I dated and time-stamped the photos Jaycen took of me, then put them in a file. Jaycen was in the other room doing his work. I heard him yelling at people over the phone more than a few times.

I could feel him watching me and couldn't stop my smile. He moved toward the bed, crawled up my body, and gently nipped the back of my thighs. I closed the laptop and laid my head down to enjoy him. His lips were soft and warm as he kissed the skin just above my silky pants. "Roll over, Angel." It was easy in the space between us. My chest was even with his mouth. "Fucking perfect," he moaned when he saw my nipples poking against the fabric of the t-shirt. His kiss was slow and torturous, sensual, and so fucking sexy, my core ached. "I have to go to the office. Will you be all right?"

Licking my lips, I smiled at him. "I have plenty to keep me busy. But I'm hungry, so would you order me some food before you go?" I touched his face; he was so good looking.

"I will, and I will wait for it before I leave. Don't answer the door, okay? No one knows that I'm staying here, so there should be no reason for someone to knock on that door."

I couldn't help but giggle. "I do have a gun, you know, and I know how to use it."

He reached up and touched my face. "Yeah, like your self-defense course?"

The laugh that escaped from me was hearty. I hadn't laughed like that in years. His smile reached his ears as he laughed with me. "Oh my God, it hurts. Go order me food and get out of here. I have work to do."

He climbed off the bed and adjusted his cock. I moaned, and he turned to smile at me. "What am I ordering?"

"Surprise me. I'll eat anything," I called out. Rolling over, I opened my laptop and continued dating and filing the pictures he took of me. I finished and closed my computer, then headed out to the living room. Jaycen was pacing the floor with the phone to his ear.

"I warned you, Sherry. He's done. I'm heading to the office to talk to the lawyers. I am breaking the contract we have with him. He's done, and I'm sorry to say this to you, but so are you." I stood there looking at him. "No, this is the fourth guy in a year. I'm done." He disconnected the call just as there was a knock on the door. He smiled at me and nodded to the bedroom, and I took my queue and went just inside the bedroom door while he opened the main door.

I stood there with a huge smile on my face, like a little girl waiting for a huge surprise. I heard the door shut, but I stayed leaning against the wall, and then he appeared in the doorway. "The food is here," he said, looking at the empty room. I didn't move; he was so beautiful. His head turned to see me leaning against the wall, and his whole demeanor changed from stern to soft. It was amazing to see. I thought right then that he liked me. Maybe I made him feel better. His body turned into mine, and he spread his legs around mine and placed his hands on my hips. "What are you doing?"

I couldn't help smiling as I tilted my head up. "Wondering what has you in such a foul mood."

"Is that what this smile is about?"

"Oh no, this smile is because you are so fucking beautiful, and I'm here with you in this hotel room. I feel like I won the lottery."

He laughed. "No, I think I'm the one who won the lottery." His hand wrapped around my neck. For some reason, I knew this move and knew he was going to kiss me. "Come on, Angel, your food is getting cold." His breath was warm on my lips. I couldn't stop myself. My arms wrapped around his neck, straining my side when he stood.

He lifted me off the floor and pulled me against his chest as he kissed me. "I'll be back as soon as I can, but chances are it won't be until late."

"I'll be fine. You go, work. If there is a problem, I'll call you. But I'm going to work and then just sleep."

He set me down, kissed my forehead, and then left. I just stood there with a stupid ass grin on my face.

Jaycen

I did not want to walk out of that hotel room, but the fucking idiots that worked for me couldn't find their dicks in the dark. I walked into the meeting room, which was filled with people and chatter. When they realized I was there, it became nearly silent. No one wanted to look at me; they knew I was pissed.

"So, tell me what the fuck is going on. Why am I here, and what the fuck is happening in L.A., because I'm pretty sure I'm not going out there. You people have worked for me for years, and it seems that now, today, hell, the past few days, everyone has forgotten how to do their fucking jobs. I am not a goddamn babysitter. I don't fucking pay you the salaries I pay you so I can micromanage your fucking jobs. My oldest friend is getting married in ten fucking days, and I'm here dealing with this shit that you people fucked up. Now, tell me why I shouldn't fire everyone in this fucking room?" In all the years I'd been doing this, I'd only ever had to treat them this way two times before. It was like they all lost their fucking minds.

My second in command cleared his throat. "Jay, the L.A. office lost six of our clients."

I snapped my head up. "Care to explain to me how the fuck that happened?"

"I don't know. It's like a virus has gotten into our system and is slowly eating us alive."

I stood there, looking at them all. "Figure it out, and figure it out fast." Walking out, I went to my office and called one of my rivals,

Steve Hartman. "Steve, it's Jay Ashford. What the hell are you doing, stealing my clients?"

He laughed. "I'm not stealing anything; they are coming to me. They said that the internal structure of your company was crumbling, that you were losing your ability to run the company." I nearly stroked out. I'd put my heart and soul into this company. It had to be Sherry. It had to be that bitch talking to my clients. "Why don't you consider letting me buy you out? I'll give you a good price for the whole lot."

It wasn't the first time he'd asked, but it was the first time I thought about considering it. Honestly, I'd had enough of the bullshit. I'd lost a relationship over this fucking life. I was getting too old to be jet-setting around, keeping tabs on adults who behaved like children. "Make me an offer." I couldn't believe the words came out of my mouth.

"What? Seriously?"

"Make me a fucking offer, and it better be reasonable. Don't think you are going to low ball me, because I have a singer in my pocket that will wipe you off the map. I'm done with this business, but if you want to fuck with me, I don't have a problem ruining you."

He laughed. "Same offer as last year."

"Sounds reasonable. Keep it between us, under the media's ears. Write it up and send it to me, and I'll look it over and get back to you."

"Are you fucking serious?"

"Do I sound serious? But if I find out you've said a word to anyone, I will sign this voice and destroy you."

"Do I get the voice in the deal?"

"Nope, she's mine."

He laughed. "Fine. I'll have the paperwork drawn up and get it to you."

I disconnected the call then called my lawyer. "We need to have a meeting, sooner rather than later. Call Heidi and set it up." There was a knock on the door. "Yeah?" I walked around and sat at my desk.

Heidi walked in. "Mr. Ashford, I have some messages for you and some mail."

I looked at my messages. "Nothing pressing." Closing my eyes, I sat there thinking about Gwyn's incredible voice and the fact that I was considering selling my fucking company. Spinning my chair around to look out the window, I didn't have a fucking clue what I was doing there. Three days earlier, I was pissed off that the woman I loved was cheating on me. I had the fourth largest recording label in the fucking country, and I was semi-happy with my life. In time, I would have gotten over Ashley. I would have buried myself in work. I was tired of working sixteen to eighteen hours a day.

I made a good living, but at what cost? I was moving closer to forty every fucking day, and I hadn't enjoyed anything. I'd traveled all over and never took the time to look where I was. Those photographs meant so much to me. They were of places I someday wanted to see, but when would that someday come? Someday was never going to happen if I kept living my life the way I had for the past ten years. Selling was a spontaneous move on my part, so out of character, I might have looked crazy. I was crazy to believe that I could have any kind of life. It had always been this stupid drive to be better, to be the best, to play King of the Hill. I'd always been an arrogant, self-centered bastard, and it took watching a woman I didn't even know getting the shit beat out of her by a man close to three times her size to wake my ass up.

Life was too short for the mad rat race of business. If I hadn't stepped in, she would probably be dead, and what a fucking shame that would have been. I knew nothing about her, yet I felt so drawn to her it scared the shit out of me. I sat there looking out of my ivory tower, when I wanted nothing more than to talk to her, banter with her, and get to know her. Was she a rebound girl? Would I have my way with her and then just walk away? No, I didn't think I would. She was too sweet. The knock on my door broke my thoughts. "Yeah?"

"Mr. Ashford, the lawyers can meet with you whenever you are ready."

"Thank you, Heidi. Ask them if they are available now, and if they will come in here."

"Of course."

I didn't even turn around; that's how arrogant I'd become. That's how important I thought myself. The knock came quickly, so I was inclined to believe that they knew something was going on.

"Yeah?" I called out, still not turning around. My eyes shifted up to see the three men walk in the door. The reflection in the glass showed somber faces. Shaking my head with a slight smile on my face, I turned around as they moved to my desk. "Gentlemen." They took up residency in the chairs in front of my desk. "Tell me what has caused these long faces?" I wanted them to tell me what they knew, but when no one said a word, I laughed. "Well, it must be bad if you aren't talking. But you know what? It doesn't matter. I need to know what we can do about these six clients that broke contracts with us. I've also fired Sherry and Ted Hicks, and I need their contracts so we can pay them out. So, get busy. I also need a recording contract for a group called The Vibe, so get me the standard. I'm going home. Deliver your findings to me here. I'll see you all on Monday. For now, I'm going to plan a bachelor party." I stood, dismissing them, then headed out. "Heidi, if any more paperwork shows up, please call me. I'm going home. I've got a busy weekend ahead of me."

She nodded, and I left with my messages in my hand. Once in the car, I called Kyle Long, the lead singer of the Vibe. "Kyle, this is Jay Ashford. Did you get me some copies of your originals?"

"We did. I have a CD of them right here."

"Do you have electronic copies? My email is on the card I gave you. Send them to me, and I'll listen to them over the weekend. If I like them, I'll call you, and we can arrange a meeting for next week."

"Really? Of course, I'll do it right now."

I chuckled. "Great, we'll talk in a few days." I disconnected the call.

"Can you take me over to the gallery on Michigan?"

"Yes, sir."

Gwyn

When he left, I stood there thinking about how lucky I'd been to have had him find me. I knew we both had serious issues, and I wasn't stupid enough to believe that Gavin would just let me go. I think, deep in my mind, I wanted Jaycen to fight for me. I wasn't sure he would. Watching a woman get the shit beat out of her would cause any man to react; he was just being a gentleman. Nothing more than what we had would come out of it. Hell, I knew I was the rebound girl from his long-time relationship. I needed to accept the fact that if I slept with him, that's all it would be. No re-bound woman lasted. They were just steppingstones. Maybe if I viewed him as my steppingstone, it would be easier.

Pushing off the wall, I ate and then went back to my computer. I needed to get through the hundreds of pictures I'd taken of Kyle and the guys. I got some great shots. I picked ten out of the ones I went through and sent them to Kyle with a note.

Hey Kyle,

I picked these for your promo. Let me know if you like them or not. I have a great many more, and I'm not doing anything these days, so I'm free to go through the others.

Talk soon,

Gwyn

After putting everything away, I dropped my clothes and went to bed.

CHAPTER SEVEN

JAYCEN

We pulled up in front of the gallery, and it looked like there was an event going on. As I got out of the car, cameras were flashing in my face. Just as I reached the door, Ashley came out of nowhere, looping her arm in mine as cameras went off. I pulled my arm away from her, and not saying a word, I walked into the gallery.

She followed me. "Jay, I can't believe you remembered. Thank you for coming. I wasn't sure how I was going to explain why you weren't here."

I honestly had no fucking idea what she was talking about. "I'm not here to see you, Ashley. I don't give a shit."

"What? This event was on our calendar."

I laughed as I moved away from her. "We don't have a calendar." I found Aubrey Jones, the owner.

"Aubrey."

"Jay, I'm glad you came."

"To be honest, I didn't remember this event was going on." I was being honest. I had no fucking idea what either of them was talking about. "I just came by to see the new photographs you have by Knight. I wanted to see if any of them spoke to me."

She smiled, looping her arm in mine. "As a matter of fact, I have twelve more. I haven't hung them yet; they are in my office. Care to see them?"

I laughed. "I would very much like to see them." I knew she wanted me, and I knew to go into her office would only escalate her flirting. But I didn't care. There was no way I was going to fuck this woman, not with the woman waiting for me at the hotel. When we walked into her office, she shut the door, and I heard her lock it, which made me smile.

"They're over here." She moved past me to the far side of the room, where a bunch of prints were lined against the wall.

"My God, they are stunning," I mumbled. I spent a good twenty minutes looking at them, with her standing inches behind me, sometimes next to me so I could see her legs in her high heels. I just smiled. *No way, sweetheart. You don't come close to what's waiting for me.* Standing slowly so I didn't brush my ass against her, I told her, "I'll take these two." I pointed to the two I wanted.

"Do you want me to deliver them?" She cooed as she moved closer to me.

I didn't want to piss her off by laughing, so I smiled instead. "I'm in transition. I'll take them with me if that's all right."

"Of course, it's all right. But I can deliver them wherever you are staying."

She was persistent. "It's fine. I'll take them with me."

I watched her move to her desk to write a bill of sale, then she handed it to me. Pulling my wallet out of my pocket, I handed her my credit card. Twenty minutes later, I was moving through the crowd with my two prints.

Just outside the door, Ashley approached me. "Jay, are you leaving already?"

I chuckled, handing the prints to my driver. Turning to her, I leaned down so not to embarrass her and whispered in her ear, "Stay the fuck away from me, Ash. I want nothing to do with you." I turned then and smiled at the camera then got in the car. I wasn't going to let her get under my skin. She wasn't worth it to me.

When I walked into the hotel room, I went right to my room and placed my new prints on the dresser with the other two, then sat on the bed to look at them. They were perfect. My mind could place me in those places. I wanted to travel to places like those in the photos, to sit and ponder the beauty. I'd lived in a concrete jungle my whole life. If Ashley hadn't done what she did to me, I would have married her. I would have never had these feelings. My eyes move to the door. I would have never known a woman like the one sleeping in the other room.

I found myself standing in her doorway, looking at her tiny, naked, bruised body, half-covered with the sheet. She was sleeping in the middle of the bed. I wanted to go touch her, kiss her. I wanted to sink into her. Instead, I went back to my room and crashed.

Gwyn

Picking up the phone that was sitting on the table next to the bed, I looked at the time. "Four-fifteen." I got up and used the bathroom, then grabbed the robe and put it on. I wanted something to drink. All the lights were off, and I couldn't help but wonder if he had returned. I walked over to the doorway, and there he was, lying on his stomach, naked, with his leg bent out to the side. Fuck if he didn't look delicious.

I felt my feet moving, and before I knew what I was doing, my hand was gently moving up his bent leg. When I crawled on the bed, I felt his breathing change; he was awake now. When my hand reached his hip, I gently pressed on it, so he would turn a bit more on his side. As I laid down, what a fucking sight I was given. His cock was semi-hard, and I wanted so badly to believe that it was because of me, but I knew men got erections when they first woke up.

But there it was, and it was fucking beautiful. Moving my head, I took his crown in my mouth and gave it a little suck. I wanted a taste. I heard him moan. "Angel, what are you doing?" His voice was rough.

"Shh." Wrapping my hand around his base, I felt his steely length grow in my hand. I wanted to give this man an orgasm that would blow his mind, just like he'd given me. I bit my tongue so my mouth would get moisture in it because it was dry as hell from nerves. I was terrified that I was actually doing this to a man I'd only known for two days.

I took him slowly into the warm, wet cavern of my mouth, gently working him further and further in until he hit the back of my throat. I knew I could take more of him. Closing my eyes, I breathed through my nose and pressed slowly until my throat relaxed, and he slid past.

Letting go of him, I put my hand on his marvelous ass and gently pressed on it, and he knew what to do. Of course, he did. He'd probably done it plenty of times. Slowly, he rocked his hips back and forth and fucked my mouth, and I felt his muscles tense. "Angel, I'm going to come." My hand firmly grabbed his ass, and I stopped him from moving, then I swallowed. His cry was a guttural moan, and I felt the warmth of him as I slowly pulled back to let him fill my mouth. When he finished and his body calmed, I pulled off him. Getting off the bed, I left his room.

I grabbed a bourbon, swallowing it down, and went back to my room, where I crawled in bed with a huge smile on my face.

Jaycen

She startled the shit out of me when I finally woke up to feel her hand on my hip. What the hell was she doing? When her warm mouth wrapped around my crown, I knew what she was doing. Holy shit. I didn't want her like this, not yet, but yeah, I was a fucking asshole and let her. Jesus, I hadn't had a decent blow job in a long time. My God, she was fucking heaven. When she made me come, I thought I was going to die.

So slow and sweet, she drew it out of me, taking her time. Fuck, when she swallowed and opened her throat for me, I swear to you I fell in love with her right there. I had never been with a woman who could swallow my cock. Hell, I'd dreamed of this shit, but I never believed it to be the truth.

When she finished, I watched her get up and leave without ever saying a word. I laid there looking at her like she was a ghost in a white robe, walking out of my room. I didn't know if I felt embarrassed or shocked. She just took what she wanted and walked away. Finally, I gained my ability to think straight and walk, so I grabbed my boxers and headed out into the living room, but it was empty. "What the fuck?" When I looked in her room, she was in bed in the same position she'd been in when I got back. *Did I just dream that? Was that real? It had to be fucking real.* The robe was on the bench, but I couldn't remember if it had been there before or not. I was definitely confused. As I walked past the alcohol, I saw a glass sitting on the shelf. Pushing my finger in, I felt that it was wet. My head jerked to the doorway; it wasn't a dream. Before I knew what I was doing, I was on the bed with her on my thighs. "What was that?" I whispered. My hands fought with my brain not to touch her. She didn't say anything, just looked into my eyes. I could've got lost in them. Her hand moved slowly up my arm to my face, to my lips. My eyes drifted closed as she trailed her fingers along my mouth.

"You're so beautiful." Her breath was hot as she kissed me.

I gently pulled her to me, her beautiful chest pressing against mine. The kiss was so perfect, sweet, slow, and long. She pulled back, her eyes locking on mine. "I thought I was dreaming," I whispered.

Her smile was slow. "I think all of this is a dream." I watched her lick her lips. "I'm the rebound girl in your life, as you are mine. I don't expect anything once this is over. But I didn't want it to end without sharing that with you."

My heart felt for this woman. Her face, though still bruised, was so beautiful. I shook my head. "You are not a rebound for anything. My relationship with Ashley has been over for months, as yours with him has been. We are not rebounding."

Licking her lips, she moved closer. Her breath on my lips smelled of bourbon. "Then, what are we?"

I brought my hand up to wrap around her neck. "We are new. Why did you come into my room, Angel?" I brushed my lips across hers.

"Please, Jaycen," she moaned.

I knew the timing was wrong. I kissed her, laying her back on the bed. "Tell me what you want, Angel."

Her back arched, and her tits were perfect with her rock-hard nipples. "Please, touch me. Taste me."

God forgive me, but listening to her beg me turned me on. My gaze moved to her nipples, and my mouth watered at the thought. Slowly, I moved down, bringing my mouth less than an inch from one. "This, Angel?"

Her hips moved. "Mmm, yes. Please," she moaned.

My tongue jetted out to brush across the hardened tip. She cried out, and her body shivered. I did the same to the other. With her hands above her head, I engulfed the perfectly round nub. Sucking it into my mouth felt like heaven. Her moans sounded low and guttural. I couldn't stop, nor did I want to stop. I nipped them, sucked them, licked them. When I raised my head to kiss her, she moaned in my mouth. "More." I couldn't help but smile.

"More what, Angel?"

Her hands cupped my face. Her eyes were dilated, searing into mine. God, the woman made me feel alive. "Please." Her mouth covered mine. I knew what she wanted; at least, I hoped I knew.

Smiling at her, I moved my hand to her hip and pressed my fingers into her ass cheeks. "Is this what you want, Angel?" Her eyes rolled in her head as my thumb pressed into her pelvic bone.

"Please."

Moving down, I clamped onto one of her nipples, gently tugging on it with my teeth. Her back came off the fucking bed as she cried out. I took my time, gently biting her as I moved down her bruised body. Cupping her tits, God, my hands were full of her. I felt her knees moving up and down in anticipation of what I was going to do to her. As I fixed myself between her legs, she rested the backs of her knees on my arms. "God, Angel, look at you." She was wide open to me, and I nearly lost my mind. I knew it wasn't the time for this, and I knew there would be serious repercussions, but hell, I wanted to taste her. Slowly, I wrapped my lips around her hood then sucked it between my lips, my tongue lifting it to find the prize. Her bud was so swollen, like her fantastic nipples. When I pressed my tongue flat and slowly licked up her sensitive flesh, she lost it. Her fingers gripped my shoulders, her nails digging in as she released. I slipped my tongue just inside her to feel her release, and she pulsed and pulsed, crying out with her pleasure.

I'd never felt this. I'd never cared about it before, and I wasn't about to stop now. I took everything she had to give. Three times she screamed out, three times she shattered under my assault. Three times it took to sedate her, which only fueled me. I wanted another, and another. She was heaven, purely divine, and I knew then that I would make her mine. As I moved up her body, her toes grasped my boxers and pulled them down. My cock was swollen and heavy as it landed on her soft skin. I slid it through her folds, relishing the slickness, then gave a little push to pop the head just inside her. "I want all of you, Angel."

Her hands pressed on my ass, pushing me a bit further. "Take me. Take all of me, Jaycen."

"There is no going back if we do this. I want all of you from this night on."

"Yes, please, Jaycen. Please."

She was begging again, and it went straight to my cock as I pushed all the way inside her. "Jesus, Angel." She was so tight. Her silky heat surrounded me, taking me to a plane of euphoria I had never know. When I was balls deep, I stopped, waiting for her to assimilate around me. Her eyes locked with mine. "Fuck, you are beautiful." My hands gripped her face gently as I kissed her, then I slowly pulled back and pushed all the way in again. She felt like heaven. I made love to her. It had been a long time since I'd taken my time to ravish a woman. She made me feel something I thought was gone. The longer we moved together, the faster I thrust. I was balls deep in this tiny woman in my arms, and I wanted more of her. Wrapping my arm around her, I pulled us up so she was sitting on my cock. I'd never had a more beautiful experience as we came together. Our moans and our breath mixed together as our mouths tangled with one another's.

She climbed off me and went to the bathroom. I didn't know what to do. I knew I'd crossed a line, so I just sat there on my heels and waited for her to come out. She climbed on the bed, then taking my hand, she pulled me down with her and nestled into my side. We didn't say a word; we just wrapped ourselves around one another.

Gwyn

Oh my God. Oh my fucking God. Never before. I only had Gavin to compare to this man, but oh my God. I wanted him so bad. Gavin never gave me an orgasm with his mouth. Three fucking orgasms in a row, and then again with his beautiful cock. *Jesus, I could seriously get attached to him.* I didn't know what to say or what to do, so I just pulled him down onto the bed with me. As I laid there in his arms, I could feel his heart slamming in his chest. *Should I talk to him? Should I just go to sleep?* I'd never had this. With Gavin, it was just sex—no cuddling, no talking—and five minutes after, he would be snoring. I sat up, pulled my knees to my chest, and looked at him. His hand moved to touch my leg.

"What's wrong?" he asked softly.

I could feel tears coming, but I didn't want to cry. I got off the bed, grabbing the robe, and left the room. I needed a drink, big time. He followed me out. Taking the glass from me, he set it down and picked me up before walking back to his room, where he climbed on the bed. "Talk to me."

"I've never done that before," I whispered.

"Done what? Had sex with someone you hardly knew?"

I giggled. "You're only the second man I've ever slept with. I've never done that," I raised my eyebrows, "before."

His face said it all. This is all that it would ever be. He didn't want anything more. My heart broke at the realization. I wanted to act tough, but I couldn't right then. I felt crushed.

"You've only been with one man?" I nodded. "And you've never had a man give you oral before?" I shook my head. "Why did you do that to me? Why did you ask me?"

"You're so beautiful, and you are so sweet to me. I thought... Well, you don't want to know what I was thinking. It's fine. It was beautiful, and I had a very good time." I went to move off his legs, but he held me firm.

"It was fine?" he choked out.

"Jaycen, I may be a bit inexperienced in the sex department, but I'm not a stupid woman. Well, some people might think otherwise. I did stay in a relationship with a man who beat me up for two years. But it was the way I was raised. For me, it was normal, or, at least, I thought it was normal. I'm not stupid to think that this, what we are doing here, is going to amount to a long-term relationship. I wanted to have sex with you before I have to leave and go back to my life, back to fighting all the time."

"Wait a minute. Who said this was over? I never did. When I came home tonight, you have no idea how much it meant to see you sleeping in there. Why are you ending something that just started?"

When I moved this time, he let me go. I got up and paced next to the bed. "We don't even know each other. How is that going to look to people? I mean, you must have friends and family. I know mine is going to shit when they find out that you are the man who beat the shit out of Gavin. It's crazy! It would be crazy stupid for me to think that we were going to last beyond next week. I slept with you because I wanted to know what it was like to be with someone who took care of me. I've never had that, so thank you." I went to walk out of his room when the prints on the dresser stopped me short. "What the fuck?" I said louder than I wanted to.

"I bought them tonight. When I got to the gallery, my ex was there. Apparently, there was a showing, and we were supposed to go together. She pretended like I was there for her. But I wasn't. Then the gallery owner made several moves on me in her office while I looked at the twelve prints she had. She even locked the door so no one could walk in. But the whole time, I just kept thinking about you being here, waiting for me. I was so pissed off, but when I saw you sleeping, it all went away. It was you I wanted, not them."

"Aubrey came on to you?" I smiled. She was such a slut.

"How do you know Aubrey?"

"She's a friend of mine. How do you know Aubrey?"

"Through the gallery."

"Humph." I walked out of his room. I wanted to tell him that those were my prints, but then he would know who I was.

"What do you mean, humph? What is it about those prints?"

I turned around and looked at him, figuring I might as well put it all out there. I put my hand out, and he took it, so I pulled him into my room. I grabbed my laptop and opened it. Opening the file that those prints were in, I clicked on one he'd just bought.

He looked at me, then the computer. "How do you have these?"

"They're mine," I whispered.

I watched his face fill with confusion. I wasn't sure I'd ever seen a man so perplexed. His fingers brushed through his hair. "You took those?" I nodded. "But your name is James."

I shook my head. "No one knows. No one."

His eyebrows crinkled. "Why?"

"I wouldn't know where to start."

"Try."

I took a deep breath, then shut down the computer and set it on the bench. "When we were little, I hated Tom, especially when he would make me call him Daddy. Every night after he went to sleep, I would steal a dollar or two from his wallet. I would take money from my mom as well, and I hid it. When I got enough to buy a camera, I did and hid that, too. He would beat us when we were bad. Sometimes, he would beat us just because he could. I started taking pictures of the marks he left on us. Then I would steal money to have the film developed." I smiled. "We used to ride the bus out of his jurisdiction in case someone reported the pictures. I've kept records of everything he did to us. When I got older, I would babysit for money and bought better cameras. It just sort of became a hobby of mine. After a while, I realized that I had a bit of talent. They offered a photography class in school, so I took it. When I went to college, I took photography classes without them knowing. I have a degree in journalism, and that's how I met Gavin, but he made me quit so I couldn't write stories about him."

He sat there looking at me. "What's with Knight?"

I smiled. "That's my name. Gwendolyn Elizabeth Knight. He wouldn't adopt us, because then we would be his responsibility, and he wasn't going to raise some other bastard's children as his own. Even though my father was his partner. I personally think he had a hand in the death of my father, but I can't prove it. But I always suspected it. I also believe that he and Gavin are dirty. That is something I can prove."

"So, the cover of *Time*, that's about you?" I nodded. "And no one knows this about you?" I shook my head. He sat there looking at me. "What's on the hard drive?"

"All the pictures, with dates and times, throughout the years of all the times he beat us, marked us. It also has photos of all my and my sister's marks."

"Why haven't you done anything about it?"

"Because my sister begged me not to. She said the repercussions would be horrendous, especially for our mother. I've seen what he can do firsthand, and I can't hurt my mom like that. I told you how sorry I am for dragging you into this."

"You didn't drag me. I think I ran full force into it. But this isn't about me. This is about three women who have been tortured. Gwyn, this is a story that has to be told."

"I can't be the one to tell it. None of the pictures have our faces on them."

"But there are scars left behind."

"I didn't tell you so you would get involved. I don't want you to save me. I have to save myself. They can and will destroy you. I only told you because you asked about my photos. That's all, Jaycen. You can't do this."

He pulled me into his embrace. "I know, Angel, but I will not let you go back there."

"But I have to. I only ever stay away for a few days after he hits me. My father will have people looking for me. I have to go back tomorrow. I think that's why I wanted this with you. I think that's why I seduced you. Because I wanted to know what it felt like to be cared for."

"There has to be another way."

"I have to go. I have a family obligation this coming weekend. It's a huge event, and I cannot miss it."

"Will he be there?"

I laughed. "Oh, yes, he will. He and Tom are the best of buds. He won't hurt me again. He wouldn't want it to go public. I'll be fine."

"Angel, I'm not sure if I can do this." He pulled me tighter.

"Jaycen, you don't owe me anything. I know that this is all it's going to be." My hand touched his face as I looked into his eyes filled with worry. "Maybe in another place, another time, things could be different. But I won't let them destroy you. I think I might like you a bit too much to let that happen."

He wrapped his hand around my neck and covered my lips with his to engage in one of his beautiful kisses. "Angel, I know I like you too much to just let you go. I don't want to let you go."

I wanted this man again. God help me.

❧

Jaycen

Holding her, making love to her was not something I was willing to give up. I couldn't bring myself to watch her walk out the door, but I knew she had to go. I wished things were different. I wanted this woman in my life. I sat there watching her pack her things, only slightly freaking out. "Will you have dinner with me tomorrow night?"

She smiled, moving over to stand between my legs. "I'm not so sure that would be the wisest decision." Her hands cupped my face.

"Why?" The word came out strangled by my fear and grief that she was leaving.

"Jaycen, I can't drag you into this. They will destroy you." She put her forehead on mine. "I want to say yes. With all that I am, I want my life to be different, but it's not. I'm not worth what will happen to you."

I wrapped my arms around her, pulling her on top of me as I laid back on the bed. "I think you are worth it. Angel, this can't be the end of this."

"It was three wonderful days, three days I will never forget. Three days that changed me, three days that have given me more strength than I've ever had. I'm not afraid anymore. I know that there are good men out there in the world, and now I have something more to fight for. Thank you for this, for caring, for treating me like a goddess, for giving me orgasms, for buying me beautiful bras and panties. Every time I put them on, I will think of you."

"I don't think I can do this, Angel. I don't think I can let you go." My hands were in her hair. It was the first time I'd ever felt this.

Her mouth covered mine. "I don't want you to ever let me go. I want to stay here like this with you."

"Then stay."

She kissed me again, then pushed up and moved away. "I can't. I really can't. But if you want, you can come with me next week. I'm leaving Sunday to go out to the Grand Canyon to shoot pictures for a week. Oh, will you hold on to this for me?" She handed me her external hard drive.

My heart jumped. "I'm your man."

She giggled. "Then it's a date. Sunday at O'Hare, nine a.m., American."

"I'll do you one better. Midway, my plane."

She turned. "You own your own plane?"

"Yep, one of the perks of being rich." I wiggled my eyebrows at her.

"Midway it is. Bring jeans and a good pair of hiking boots. You should probably break them in before you put them on out there. Get them wet and wear them until they dry. That way you won't get blisters." She picked up her bags. "I'm ready."

My heart hurt. I hadn't even felt this way when Ashley cheated on me. "Please be safe. I'll be here if you need me. You have my number. Use the burner phones if you're worried about them keeping tabs on you."

"I don't care if they do or not." She put her hand on my chest and looked up into my eyes. "I've got something to fight for."

"Fucking straight, you do."

"Don't forget me." Her eyes looked sad.

"Not in a million fucking years, Angel. Not in a million years."

She gave me her beautiful smile and turned to walk out the door. I followed her, but she didn't look back. She continued right out of the hotel room door. I felt an emptiness swallow me whole. It had been only three days, and I felt more for this woman than I ever did for Ashley. Three days, and my life had been changed forever. For the first time in my life, I hoped she would call. But I knew she wouldn't. She was a strong woman, and she was fighting for her freedom. I had no other choice but to let her.

Gwyn

Leaving was so hard. I wanted to go back. I wanted to stay with him. I turned at the elevator, forcing myself to stay there. I couldn't hurt him. I knew what was coming. I knew the fight I had ahead of me. I had the same fight every single time. First, my father, then with my sister and mother, and then Gavin would show up to say how sorry he was. He would promise to never hurt me again. Until the next time it happened, and it would happen again. If Jaycen hadn't stopped him, I believe he would have seriously hurt me, if not killed me. I would end this mess, and I would do it the right way.

The elevator doors opened, and when I turned to push the button, he was standing there looking at me. His arm reached out and grabbed me around the waist, his mouth crashing down on mine. His kisses were the best. Pulling back, he touched my face. "Don't forget me, Angel."

"It'll never happen. I will see you Sunday at Midway." He smiled and let me go. I swear to God, it took everything I had to leave this man. But I had to go. I had to do this. Stepping back, I pushed the button, and the doors closed. My heart sank. Closing my eyes, I breathed in and prepared myself for what was to come.

Jaycen

That was the single most difficult thing I'd ever done in my life. I had one week to get my affairs in order because, no matter what she thought, I was not letting her go after Sunday. I was on a mission. I needed to go find some hiking boots and whatever other gear I might need. Grabbing my wallet, keys, and my phone, I headed out. I took a cab and ended up at Moosejaw. I was fitted for a very expensive pair of hiking boots and bought a backpack. The girl who helped me acted as if she thought I was nuts. She showed me knives, picks, and a few other things. I bought a rope, a first aid kit, a canteen, two heavier shirts, and some good socks. All in all, it was a productive day.

When I got back to the hotel, I decided to just focus on work. I needed to get that contract signed for The Vibe before I sold out to Hartman. Turning on my computer, my inbox was flooded with emails. It took me nearly two hours to get through them all. The same with my phone. So many messages. Jesus, this was what three days did to a company when the boss wasn't there. To be honest, I was looking forward to not doing this anymore. I wanted out more than I realized. If I had nothing to lose, they couldn't hurt me. They couldn't destroy me like she thought they would.

CHAPTER EIGHT

GWYN

Walking into my apartment, just like I did every other time he fucking hit me, was the same. Notes were left on the tables, apologies, flowers. As I moved through my apartment, picking up the notes, I threw them away. I turned on my phone and called downstairs to arrange for the flowers to be sent to the children's hospital. I didn't want a fucking thing from the asshole. Sitting with my cameras on the coffee table, I assessed the damage. I would need two new lenses and a new camera. The ring was broken off. I grabbed my bag and headed out to the camera store. When I opened my door, Gavin was standing there. I fucking knew it.

"Gwyn, you're all right." He had two black eyes and a bandage on his nose. I nearly laughed, just knowing Jaycen beat the shit out of him.

"I'm just on my way out. What do you want, Gavin?"

"Please, baby, I don't know what came over me. I am so sorry for hurting you, but just seeing that fucker with his hands on you made me crazy. You're mine."

Closing the door, I shook my head. "No, Gavin, I'm not yours. I haven't been yours for a long time. You need to stop this shit. I'm not coming back."

I moved around him, and he grabbed my arm. "You. Are. Mine." He growled as he pulled me to him. He spun me around, and the palm of my hand slammed him in the face. He let me go, screaming in pain as blood poured out of his nose.

"I don't belong to you. Stop coming around here, Gavin." I turned and made my way to the elevator. I could hear him mumbling, calling me a fucking bitch. I tried with all that I had not to laugh. When I turned in the elevator, he was standing by my door, looking at me. I just shook my head as the doors closed. When I got to the lobby, I stopped to let the concierge know that there was blood all over the carpet outside my door, and could they please clean it up.

Outside, I grabbed a cab and headed to my father's office. I didn't bother waiting to be announced; I just walked in the door. He was in a meeting with a few people. "Gwendolyn." He stood, looking at the men seated in front of his desk. "Would you please excuse us? I need to speak to my daughter." I nearly laughed; I wasn't his daughter.

I moved out of the doorway while they left, then I shut the door and spun around. "You need to do something about fucking Gavin. Do you see my face? He did this to me as he slammed my head into the concrete outside of The Jewel. He was going to kill me."

"From my understanding, you were all over some guy there."

"Are you fucking serious? I broke up with Gavin three months ago because he thinks it's all right to beat me up. I hugged a friend. I swear to God, if you don't stop him, I will. I'm not going to live like this, not anymore."

He moved quickly and was in my face. "Do not threaten me, little girl."

I didn't know where the braveness came from, but I pushed against his chest. "I will do what is necessary to protect myself from you and from him. You are not my father. You are just like him, a fucking monster." I put my hand on the doorknob and opened the door. "Touch me again, and I am filing criminal charges against you, the same for Gavin Highland. I am not a fucking punching bag. I'm done, Daddy. I'm done letting you beat me. I'm twenty-six years old, and I will fight back." I turned and made it maybe two steps before he grabbed my arm. We were in front of about twenty people. When he turned me around, I swung, hitting him in the face with the heel of my hand. "No. No means no! You are not going to hurt me again." He let go of me, and I walked to the elevator. My eyes moved to the shocked faces, and I told them, "My father, the Police Commissioner, is a physically abusive man. So is Gavin Highland, the same Gavin Highland that is running for District Attorney. He did this to my face." My father stood there, a horrified look on his face. I turned and looked at him. "This ends now, or I will destroy you. Keep him away from me." I was physically shaking when I made it to the elevators. Reaching into my bag, I searched for one of the burner phones. I pulled out my wallet as the phone loaded, then I got in the elevator and left. Once I made it out to the street, I dialed his number.

"Jaycen Ashford."

I couldn't talk. I just started to cry.

"Angel?" I nodded. "Sweetheart talk to me. Are you okay?"

"I-I..."

"Breathe. Where are you? I'll come and get you."

"No. Are you at the hotel?"

"Yes."

"Okay." I disconnected the phone. Walking down the street, I found a cab and headed to the hotel. I had him drop me off a block away and walked the rest of the way. In the lobby, I picked up a phone and called his room. "I'm here."

"Go to the desk and tell them you are Angel, and they will give you a key to the elevator."

When I knocked on his door, he whipped it open and pulled me into his arms. Lifting me off the floor, he turned us into the room. I was still shaking. "What the hell happened?" he whispered as he held me close. Shaking my head, I just cried. I didn't want to be weak, but I was freaking the hell out of myself. I knew how bad it was going to be for my mother. Jaycen carried me to the couch and sat me down, then went to get a drink for me. He handed me a bourbon, and I downed it. After a few minutes, I got control and proceeded to tell him what I'd done. He smiled the whole time.

"Good for you. I swear to God, Angel, if he hurts you again, I'm going to kill him."

"You won't have to. I think, after what I did today at Tom's office, Gavin won't come near me. He knew I was serious. I'm sure I just ruined my relationship with my mother and sister. But you know what?" He shook his head. "I don't fucking care anymore."

"What can I do?" He looked so worried.

I smiled at him as I reached to touch his face. "You're doing it. I'm sorry for dragging you into this mess."

"Hey, stop it. You didn't drag me in."

"I should go. I was on my way to the camera store. One of my cameras is broken, and I need to get another one."

"Do you want me to come with you?"

I shook my head. "No. I shouldn't have come here, but I just needed…" I couldn't say it.

"Needed a friendly face?"

My hand touched his cheek, and I nodded. "A safe place. A place I knew I wouldn't be hurt. A place I didn't fear being."

He tilted his face into my hand, his hand covering mine. "I will always be here."

I got up and made my way to the door. Looking in his room when I passed by it, I saw all the bags and smiled. "You went shopping," I smarted.

"Yep, needed to get some new boots." He was behind me. As I turned, he wrapped his hand around my neck and kissed me. "I have a date to spend a week with this incredible woman that I met."

"Jaycen," I whispered.

"Yes, Angel?"

"Thank you."

He nodded, letting me go. I left with a smile on my face and headed to the camera store.

Jaycen

Watching her repeatedly walking out my door was taking its toll on me. I admittedly had become seriously attached to this woman. I wanted her with me always. I couldn't explain it and was unsure if I wanted to try. I just knew that when she left, I felt it.

It felt incredible knowing it was me she'd called when she was afraid, when she was distressed. I was beyond ecstatic, knowing it was me that calmed her inner storms when she was upset. I needed to just finish this life so that they couldn't hurt me, so I would be free to spend every chance I got with her.

After changing my clothes, I headed to the office. I had a week to get this done because, on Sunday, I was going to do the one thing I hadn't allowed myself in the last ten years. I was going on vacation.

Walking into the office, I was greeted by Heidi. "Mr. Ashford, I have your messages, and there are some contracts on your desk. Also, a courier brought a sealed envelope."

I took the messages. "Thanks, Heidi. I don't want to be disturbed."

"Yes, sir. I'm going to take my lunch."

I nodded and looked at my messages in my hand as I walked into my office then closed the door behind me. I moved to my desk, the envelope beckoning me. As I opened it, my phone vibrated. I nearly flung it across the room, trying to get it out of my pocket. Swiping it on, I answered. "Angel?"

"No, but if you want, I can get some wings." Caden's laughter bellowed through the phone.

"Fuck you, asshole. What's up?"

"Well, first, I want to know who this Angel person is."

"She's a woman I met over the weekend."

"You bringing her to the wedding?"

"Oh, fuck no. I know for a fact that Ashley is going to be there."

"Seriously, you think she'll actually show up?"

"Oh, I know she will. I stopped by the gallery to look at some prints the other night. There was a showing going on, and she was there, looking for me. She said it was on our calendar. So, your nuptials are on the calendar. No, I'm not bringing anyone."

"Well, that's why I'm calling. I know you have the tux, but did you get the matching cummerbund to go with the Maid of Honor's dress?"

"I haven't been home. I'll go by there after work and see if it's there. Hey, when do I get the rings?"

He laughed. "Tomorrow night at dinner. Don't forget."

"What does your brother think of not being the best man?"

"Yeah, he was pissed, but I bought him a Porsche, so he's over it."

I started laughing. "No fucking shit, you bought him a Porsche? Wow, that's a bit extreme, even for you."

"Yeah, but I am only doing this once in my life, and I want my best friend to be my best man. It was totally worth it."

"So, is this what you called me for?"

"Yeah, but now I want to know who this Angel is."

I laughed. "Not on your life, asshole."

"Whatever. So, I'll see you tomorrow night for dinner. Ally is going out with some friends, so it should be a good time."

I knew what he was saying. "You are such a dick."

"Fuck you, I'm getting married. I am going to have sex with the same woman for the rest of my life. I am just doing what tradition says."

"Yeah, well, how would you feel if Ally did the same?"

"Fuck that, her cunt belongs to me."

"Well, wouldn't the same go for her, that your dick belongs to her?"

He laughed. "Nothing belongs to her until I put that ring on my finger, and even then, she needs to deserve it."

"You are fucked up, you know that, right?"

"Yeah. Listen, I gotta go. Tomorrow night, and check on the cummerbund."

"Yeah, whatever."

I disconnected the call. "What a dick." I would never sleep with another woman days before my wedding.

Pushing him out of my head, I tore open the envelope. I read through the contract. Two-hundred and fifty million was a good, sound offer, so I made sure everything was on point and that there were no hidden deals within the pages. An hour later, I picked up my pen and signed my company away. I didn't hesitate. I knew I was done fighting the fight. Setting the contract aside, I put on my headphones and listened to the demo that The Vibe had sent over. They were good. I sent Kyle an email and told him to come in as soon as they could to discuss a contract. I was surprised when he responded right away.

Mr. Ashford,

We are available whenever you are. Just let me know.

Thanks again,

Kyle Long

Laughing, I told him to be at my office in an hour. I wanted them signed before I sold. I promised Caden I would give them a chance. My phone pinged. Grabbing it up, I had a text from an unknown number. Swiping it open, I found it was from her.

~Thank you for earlier today. No more unexpected visitors. I got a new camera and am looking forward to Sunday. Hey, does your plane (Mr. Rich) have a bed in it? ~

~Anytime, Angel, and yes, it does. Why? ~

~Have you ever used it? ~

I had to laugh. She wanted to know if I'd had sex in my plane's bed.

~Yes. ~

~Oh. ~

I laughed. She was so cute.

~To sleep. ~

She sent a dancing emoji. *~Good to know. ~*

I just laughed and set my phone down. I continued to work until the band arrived. We sat and discussed the contract and what was required of them and the rules of engagement. Three hours later, with the contract signed and the recording dates set, they left, and I had Heidi call me a messenger. When the day was done, I headed to my apartment to pick up my cummerbund then took it upstairs to put with my tux.

Walking into this place felt weird. It no longer felt like home. As I moved through the place to what had once been mine and Ashley's room, I heard giggling. I flipped the switch, and sure enough, there she was in my new bed with the same guy. "What the fuck are you doing here?" I shouted.

The guy rolled off her and landed on the floor. He stood up, and definitely was not wearing a condom. "Jay!"

"Get the fuck out! Just take your fucking, lying, whore ass, and get the fuck out!" I shouted.

The guy was moving past me, with his clothes in his hands. Ashley pulled the covers over her body. "No need, sweetheart. I've seen it all before. What, are you trying to get knocked up so you can claim it's mine? Get dressed, Ash, and get the fuck out."

She got up and put her clothes on. "Jay, I'm already pregnant, and it is yours."

I laughed as I moved to the closet, tossing her things out into the bedroom. I grabbed a suitcase and threw that out. "It's not mine. I had a vasectomy ten years ago. I just had a sperm count last week, and I'm shooting blanks. It's not mine. Pack your shit and get out." I grabbed a handful of her dresses and walked to the door. She stood there with her mouth open.

"You had a vasectomy? Why wouldn't you tell me that?" She was in shock. Her hand moved to brush her hair out of her eyes, and I saw the ring I'd bought her on her finger.

Reaching forward, I grabbed her hand and pulled the ring off. "Where did you fucking get this?"

"It's mine." She reached for it, but I pulled my hand back. "You bought it for me. I found it in the safe."

"How did you figure out the combination? I never gave this to you, so it's not yours."

"But you were going to give it to me. It's mine, Jay. We were meant to be together."

I shook my head. "Get out, or I'm calling the police."

"Jay, this is my home, too."

"No, it's not." I pulled my phone out of my pocket and dialed the police. "Yes, I'd like to report a break-in." I told them my address, then looked at her after I disconnected the call. "They'll be here in a few minutes. Pack your shit and get out." Walking out of the room, I went to my office and opened the safe. Everything was still there, even the box for the ring. I took it and put it in my pocket. Walking back into the bedroom, I found Ashley on the floor, crying while putting her clothes in the suitcase.

"Why would you do that, Jay? Why wouldn't you tell me?"

"Because I didn't want some slut to get pregnant and trap me or take all my fucking money. I'm so done with women like you." She just sniffled and packed. The police showed up, and I explained to them what was going on. She was escorted out with her belongings. On my way out, I stopped by the concierge and asked if they could get a locksmith up there to change the locks, then asked if they could call me when they had it done. Then I made sure Ashley couldn't get a key. This weekend was going to be a joke. I wanted to take Gwyn to Caden's wedding, but I knew fucking Ashley would be there, and I didn't want to make her uncomfortable. Although, somehow, I didn't think Gwyn would be the one feeling uncomfortable.

I just went back to the hotel and tried to crash, but thoughts of her stayed close to me. I ended up just lying in bed, thinking about the best three days of my life.

Gwyn

I had no idea what had gotten into me with this guy. He was incredible in bed, his kisses were to die for, and all I wanted to do was fuck him and spend my time with him. I was really looking forward to going away with him.

There was a knock on my door. Taking a deep breath, I grabbed the gun out of my purse then walked over to the door while shoving the gun in the back of my jeans. When I looked out, my sister was standing there with sunglasses on, which only meant one thing. That fucker had hit her again. I ripped the door open and saw the tears on her cheeks.

She threw herself into my arms, crying. "What the hell happened?" I said as I pulled her inside and closed the door behind us. She pulled back and took off her sunglasses. "Son of a bitch, that bastard. What are you doing? Why are you going to marry him?"

"Daddy said I had to. He said that he would lose all that money he'd spent on deposits. Gwyn, I don't have that much money to pay him back. I love him. I want him."

"Maybe so, but at what cost? Your life? He's hitting you in the face now. Look what fucking Gavin did to me. This isn't right. Tell me why he did this. Tell me the reason behind it."

"Because I told him I want children. He doesn't. He said they suck the life out of you and that he never wants children, and if that's the only reason I let him fuck me without a condom, then he'll quit fucking me."

"See, I don't understand why or how you would even consider bringing a child into such a volatile relationship."

"It's not that bad, Gwyn. He's getting better. He's more tender and easier in his apologies."

I shook my head and picked up my camera. She let me shoot her face then lifted up her shirt to show where he had kicked her in the side. I wanted to cry, knowing she was going to marry a fucking monster. When I finished, I pulled the memory card and slipped it into the little pocket on the front of my jeans.

"So, why are you here?" I didn't want to be rude, but I wasn't in the mood to listen to her whine about that fucker.

"I heard about what you did to Gavin."

"Jesus, what does he do, run around and cry to everyone?"

"You know they are friends, close friends."

"Yeah, and you can thank the fucker for introducing us. I should have known Gavin would be just like him."

"So, why did you hit him in the face after that guy broke his nose?"

I had to laugh. Jaycen did a number on him, that's for sure. "Because he grabbed me. I told you when I left him that I wasn't going to let him hurt me again. See what he did to me that night?" I showed her my face and thigh. "I'm done. I told Tom the same thing and that he better make sure Gavin backs off, or I'm going to destroy them both. I just want my life back. I want what I had before the fucker came into it. You shouldn't marry this asshole."

"I love him, Gwyn. I honestly love him. Will you do my makeup Saturday?"

"You know I will."

"Okay, I need to get going. Please reconsider Gavin. It's important to me that you two get along."

"Hey, as long as the fucker doesn't touch me, I'm fine with him. But I don't belong to him. If you want to have a beautiful time on Saturday, tell the fucker not to touch me."

"I will. I love you, Gwyn."

I hugged my sister. "I love you, too."

Closing my door, I leaned against it. "Fuck." This was so out of control. I wasn't sure what I wanted to do. I knew where I wanted to be, and it wasn't my apartment. Grabbing my bag and keys, I left.

After walking for a while, I stepped into a coffee shop, my eyes searching for that one person who I was sure had been hired to watch me. But no one jumped out at me. So, I got a coffee and started walking again. I made it to The Bean and sat down, and that's when I saw him. "Fucking assholes." I got up and went inside one of the little shops, where I saw a guy and walked up to him. "Could you please help me? That man over there, the one in the hat, has been following me."

He looked over my head. "Of course. I'll do whatever I can."

"Thank you. I'm kind of scared."

The guy moved around me and caused a scene with him over a pair of sunglasses. I ran out the side entrance to the street and hailed a cab. When I got in, I told him where to take me, keeping my eyes on the shop. The guy didn't come out, at least, not that I saw. When we pulled up to the hotel, I got out and ran inside, getting in the first elevator I came to. It took me to the floor below his. I got out and went to the stairs, but the door was locked, so I called him.

"Jaycen Ashford."

"Hi. I have a bit of a problem, and I was wondering if you could help me."

He laughed. "Always. What seems to be the problem?"

"I'm on the floor below you, and the door to the stairs is locked. Can you come and open it for me?"

"Be right there."

I stood at the door, waiting for him. Just as the door opened, someone grabbed me from behind. "What the fuck are you doing here?" Fucking Gavin. "Meeting your fucking lover?" He slammed me against the wall, and I kneed him in the balls, pushing him away.

"Get your fucking hands off my wife." I heard as Jaycen hit him in the side of the head. He pushed me behind him as Gavin stood up.

"Your what?" Gavin's eyes were on mine.

"My fucking wife. If you touch her again, I am filing charges. In fact, I'm calling the police now. This is the second time you've assaulted her."

Gavin laughed. "I know for a fact she isn't your wife. She is engaged to me, and I am the fucking police."

"We shall see about that." He started dialing.

"Wait, wait," Gavin said, putting his hand on Jaycen's phone. Then he looked at me. "You're married to him?"

"I told you I didn't belong to you anymore. Just leave, Gavin, and leave me alone."

"You're fucking married? When, Gwyn? When did you get married?" He was looking at Jaycen, who towered over him.

"It's none of your business."

"You're the fucker who hit me the other night."

"I am, and if it wasn't for my wife, I wouldn't have stopped. Don't fucking touch her again. Don't look at her. Don't talk to her. Don't even fucking breathe around her. Is that understood?"

He stood there, staring at me, then looked at Jaycen. My hand was on Jaycen's back. "Come on. Let's leave," I said softly. Stepping back, I moved with him, staying nicely tucked behind him as we walked to the elevator. Jaycen didn't take his eyes off Gavin. I pushed the down button, and when the doors opened, he stepped back and pushed me back with him.

When the doors closed, he turned around, pulling me into his arms. "What the fuck." I didn't say anything. I didn't know what to say. The doors opened, and he tucked me into his side as we moved through the lobby.

A beautiful brunette stepped in our path. "Jay?"

"Fuck," he whispered. I felt his body tense.

"What are you doing here?" She looked at me. "Who's this?" He didn't say anything, just moved us around her. Yep, she followed us, her heels clicking across the marble floor. "Jaycen, stop," she said. I felt her grab his arm, but he pulled away from her. We reached the elevator up to his room, and she was right there. "Who the hell is this?"

I smiled at her, then leaning in, I said softly, "I'm his wife, sweetie. Would you mind not touching him?"

I swear to God, she nearly had a stroke, standing there looking at me. Her eyes shot up to his. "You're married?"

He shook his head. "None of this is your business. Please, just leave us alone."

"Yes, please do. See, we are trying to get on with our honeymoon, and fucking idiot people just keep getting in our way."

I felt him chuckle. "Ash just go. I told you I'm done."

"But what about the baby?" She looked right at me when she said it.

I couldn't help but giggle. "Nice try." The doors opened, and we stepped in. She made a move to step inside the elevator, so I moved out of his embrace stood face to face with her. "I'm sorry, sweetie, but this is a private elevator." The doors closed on her shocked face. Jaycen swiped his key card, and it started moving.

He pulled me into his arms, his chin gently touching my head. It felt so good to be wrapped in him. God, he smelled so good. When the doors opened, we moved as one to his room. He opened the door and pulled me inside. The door slammed, and he leaned against me. "What the hell was that?"

I pushed against his chest, and he stepped back. Walking into the room, I poured two glasses of bourbon and handed him one. I swallowed the liquid down and poured another one. "My sister came over with a black eye and some serious bruises. We had a talk; I took some pictures. When she left, I just felt so horrible, and I'm tired of feeling that way, so I wanted to come over and see you because I don't feel that way here. In fact, I feel calm and safe here. Jaycen, I've been living in hell for the majority of my life, and the three days I was here with you were the most freeing I think I've ever had."

"Stay with me."

I smiled. "On my way over, I discovered some guy following me, so I asked a random guy to help me, and I got away. I jumped in a cab and headed over here. Apparently, there was more than just the one guy, because Gavin followed me up here. I didn't know which elevator to go to. You know the rest."

"You should have called me. I would have come and got you."

I sat there, looking at him. "You told him we were married." My voice was almost a whisper.

He chuckled. "That was my ex in the lobby."

"She is very beautiful. I am so sorry she hurt you the way she did."

"My scars are internal and will heal over time. Yours, however, are much deeper. It just came out. Besides beating that fucker to death, it was the only thing I could think to say to him to get him to back off. If he thinks you are my wife, it brings a whole different level of anxiety for him. He has no other choice but to not hurt you again. I'm sorry if it upset you."

I bumped his shoulder. "I really would have enjoyed watching you beat the shit out of him."

Laughing, he wrapped his arm around me and pulled me onto his lap. "Come here, wife of mine."

I couldn't help but laugh. "This is a whole new ball game. He and my father are going to search and try to have it annulled."

"Well, at least, it will keep them busy for a while. At least until Sunday, when we can get the hell out of here."

I don't know why, but I couldn't wait to be with him. My fingers touched his face. "Jaycen, thank you for being there that night. Thank you for being the one who rescued me."

"I was heading out the door, and then you opened this incredible mouth of yours and drew me right back in. But when you smiled at me, I think my heart woke up. I think I woke up." His voice sounded so gentle and kind.

I just needed to kiss him. So, I did.

CHAPTER NINE

JAYCEN

When I opened the door and saw that fucker touching her, hurting her, I lost my fucking mind. I hit him so hard, it felt like I'd broke a few bones in my hand. I told him she was my wife. I'm pretty sure that word had never come out of my mouth before. But it felt so fucking right to say. Then we ran into fucking Ashley. When Gwyn said she was my wife, my heart surged. It felt good to hear her defend me, protect me.

Laying with her in my arms, in my bed, completely naked, was the rightest feeling. Making love to her, cherishing her, was all I wanted to do. She was incredible, and she was mine. I couldn't let her go. She snuggled closer to me, and I felt compelled to pull her into my embrace.

Raising her head up, her eyes were sleepy, and she smiled a small smile before touching my lips. "What's wrong?" Her voice came out as a whisper.

"Not a thing. I just can't seem to sleep."

She pushed herself up. "Do you want to talk?"

It amazed me how attentive she was to me, to my needs. I couldn't stop the smile. "I told that man you were my wife."

"Yes, and I told your ex the same thing."

My hand rested on her thigh. "Did I do the right thing?"

Her smile melted me. "You did what you had to do to defuse the situation." I sat up, touching her face.

"But did I do the right thing? I don't want to hurt you any more than you already are." She leaned her head into my hand. "I told her I was your wife. Did I do the right thing?"

"Well, you shut her up, that's for sure. Angel, being here with you like this, making love to you, touching you, hell, just being in a room with you feels so perfect, so right. It's been, what, five days, and I feel like it's been a lifetime. That's how you feel to me."

Leaning forward, she sweetly kissed me. "I came here because I was upset, because I wanted to tell you what was going on. It's like you've been in this with me the whole time, so yes, it feels like we've never been apart. I know it's weird. It has to be weird to feel like this about someone I don't know, not really. It's almost as if our souls know one another."

"Yes, like we are two old souls reuniting. That's it."

"Jaycen, when you told him I was your wife, it felt right. I know I shouldn't say that…"

I interrupted her. "No, that's just it. When I said it, it felt right."

"What are you saying?"

I smiled. "Well, we could get married. I mean, then it wouldn't be a lie, and you could stay here with me."

She started to giggle. "That's just crazy. Who gets married after knowing someone for five days? Oh, you're crazy."

I chuckled. "I suppose. But remember when I told you that one day, I hope to be sure that I will be the last and only man you ever fuck?" She nodded. "Well, I'm sure. Are you sure? I mean, you've only been with him and me, so there are a lot of men out there for you to try on." I had no idea what the fuck I was saying. I would lose my mind if she said she wanted to explore other men.

She laughed. "Oh, I'm sure." Her body rose, and she wrapped herself around me. "I'm so sure that no man will ever kiss me like you do. I'm so sure that no man will ever touch me the way you do or hold me the way you do. I'm so sure, Jaycen, that no man will ever make love to me like you do. Don't ask me how I know this; I just do."

"And just think, I haven't even fucked you yet."

She kissed me, whispering in my mouth, "No, but I'm hopeful that one day you will."

I got lost in her again. It was so easy to forget the world outside, especially while buried inside this magnificent woman. She was so tight, so receptive to every movement we shared. Her body was mine to cherish and worship, and that's all I wanted to do. Her heart was true, and she made me feel so alive. Once we were both spent, she crawled back into bed after cleaning herself up, positioned herself over me on her hands and knees, and looked me right in the face.

"Yes. As crazy as this is, yes."

I swear to God, my heart stopped. My smile grew to the point of pain in my cheeks. Wrapping her in my arms, I pulled her down on my chest and kissed her. When we parted, I looked at her. "Yeah?"

She nodded. "Yeah." Pulling her lip between her teeth, she smiled. "We can go to Vegas."

I started laughing; I couldn't have been happier. It was the craziest thing I'd ever done, but it felt so right. "You want to go now?"

Turning her head, she looked at the clock. I turned to look and saw it was nine at night. "We could be back by morning. Do you?"

"Would I seem like a crazy man if I said yes?"

She laughed. "No crazier than me."

"If you are serious, then yes, let's do this. I just need to call my pilot."

"I really think I am, Jaycen. Are you?"

I rolled her over, touching her beautiful face, which was still covered in bruises. "Angel, it would be a privilege and an honor to make you my wife."

Her smile said it all. "Then, yes."

I had to kiss her and make love to her again. When we finished, we got dressed and headed to the airport.

∾

Gwyn

I had no fucking idea what I was doing or why. Well, I knew why. He was gorgeous and kind and caring. He protected me and didn't make me regret a damn thing. We got on his plane, and fifteen minutes later, we were flying down the runway. I'd never done this before, gotten on a private jet at the spur of the moment to do anything, let alone to get married.

"Are you one of those men who will want me to quit my job and stay home to cook and clean for you? Are you going to make me dress up like a Barbie doll and accompany you to high-powered events?" I was serious. That life was not the life I wanted.

"Not unless you want to do those things. I was more or less hoping we would spend our days and nights in bed, only coming out to eat."

I couldn't help but giggle. "I would so do that."

He leaned over and kissed my head. "I have no desire to control you, Angel."

Those words were music to my ears. I snuggled into his side and relaxed, nearly falling asleep, until a gorgeous woman spoke softly to Jaycen. "Sir, is there anything I can get you or your guest?"

My eyes fluttered open. "A bottle of water would be lovely." I saw the glare she gave me, and it made me smile.

"No, I'm good," he said to her, then turned to kiss my forehead. "Are you a jealous woman?"

I laughed. "I've never had anything to be jealous about. I probably would have paid someone to sleep with Gavin to make him leave me alone."

He was chuckling. "So, you don't get jealous?"

"Why are you asking me this?" I sat up. "Do you want me to be jealous? Are beautiful women going to be draping themselves all over you? I'm not sure I understand what you are asking me or why." He just sat there looking at me with his hazel eyes; I swear, they looked like they were dancing. The beautiful woman came over and handed me a cold bottle of water and a napkin. I thanked her, but she wasn't looking at me; her eyes were on him.

When she moved away from us, he smiled at me. "I've been in one serious relationship in my life, and you know what happened there. I was going to ask her to marry me, but I didn't. I bought a ring and everything. I never really wanted to get married because I never wanted children. Ashley never struck me as the type of woman who would ever do something that could possibly destroy her body. Not that any of that matters. I've been with a fair number of women, each of them equally as beautiful as Ashley. But none of them, and I mean none of them even come close to how beautiful you are. You are so kind, and caring, and smart. I don't think you have a manipulative bone in your body. You are strong and brave. Women come on to me all the time, but I want you to know that I will never cheat on you. When I put that ring on your finger tonight, that's it for me. You are it for me." I swallowed hard. He was so sincere. "I don't want you to feel threatened by anyone you see making a move on me, and you will see it. My eyes are on you only. I am taking this seriously, marrying you. I'm being self-ish. I may say it's so that prick leaves you alone, but it's more for me. Because I want you. I want to spend the rest of my life with you."

"We've only known each for five days." My voice sounded like that of a small child. "How could you know that?"

"Same way you know it."

I smiled. "You feel it, too?"

"I do, Angel. I absolutely do. I knew it the second I looked into your eyes on that stage. I was yours then, I am yours now, and I will be yours for the rest of your life if you'll have me."

My hand moved on its own to touch his face. "Are you for real?" I whispered.

"So real, Angel. So fucking real." His hand wrapped around my neck, and his lips found mine, and dear God, I lost my mind. Pulling back, he whispered on my lips, "So real."

We snuggled together in the seats. I must have fallen asleep because when the plane hit the runway, I woke up. A few minutes later, we were in a car and leaving the airport. We pulled up in front of the Bellagio. "There's a jewelry store here. I'd like to buy you a ring. You okay with that?"

I shook my head. "No rings yet. Let's just do this. We can get rings later."

"You sure?" I could hear the disappointment in his voice.

Turning in my seat, I climbed on his lap, straddling him and cupping his face with my hands. "Tell me why," I whispered.

"Because I want the world to know you are mine."

"But it doesn't matter to anyone but us." I kissed him.

"Angel, let me buy you a ring," he moaned in my mouth.

"I want something simple, no big diamond. A simple band."

His smile lit up the car. "A simple band," he whispered as I captured his bottom lip in my mouth. I reached over and opened the door, climbing off him and out of the car. "Well, then come on." I put my hand out.

Jaycen

I swear to God, this woman was everything I'd ever wanted. As I climbed out of the car, her smile and the sparkle in her eyes drew me in. She could ask me to do anything, and I would go with a goofy-ass grin on my face. She was about five steps ahead of me, and damn if it was the best view. Her hand out behind her, her fingers wiggled for me to catch up and hold her hand. I picked up my pace, grabbing her hand.

I leaned in. "I was looking at this fine ass of yours."

She giggled. "Well, if you're a good boy, you can have this ass on our way home." That sparked my attention. We walked into the jewelry store, and of course, because of the way we were dressed, we were snubbed.

"Excuse me, sir, but I don't think we have anything in here for you," one of the bitchy girls said to me.

I smiled at her. "Could I speak to the manager, please?"

Gwyn didn't care what the woman said. She was roaming around, looking in all the display cases. When the bitchy girl returned, a man was with her.

"I'm Mr. Gerard. How can I help you?"

"Well, Mr. Gerard, we would like to buy some wedding bands."

His face flushed. "Sir, I'm sure you could find something more affordable in perhaps a store on the street."

I reached in my back pocket and pulled out my Black card, handing it too him. "I'm sure this store will be fine." I turned and followed Gwyn over to a case. She was looking at a beautiful ruby bracelet. "Did you find a simple band?"

When she turned, her smile made my breath hitch. "I did, and I found one for you as well. But I want to pay you for it." I ran my thumb across her cheek. I wanted to kiss her, but we were interrupted.

"I'm so sorry, Mr. Ashford. Please, accept my apologies."

Without picking my head up, I said, "It's not a problem, Mr. Gerard. My future wife has found what she wants."

"Very good."

"Show him what you want, Angel," I nearly growled it out. She was so beautiful, her eyes so mesmerizing. Licking her lips, she moved away from me to a case on the other side of the room. I looked up, and the rude woman was standing there. I looked at her and said, "That ruby bracelet, I would like to purchase it. But it's a surprise." She nodded, and I walked over to where Gwyn was.

"What size ring do you wear?" She smiled at me.

"I haven't a clue." Mr. Gerard had a ring sizer and took my size. My hands were quite big. We laughed about the difference. Her ring size was five, but mine was ten. Gwyn continued to look around while I paid. After slipping the box holding the bracelet in my jacket pocket, I took the bag with our rings. I nodded to Mr. Gerard, and we left.

"So, where do you want to get married?"

I smiled. "Maybe, let's have Elvis marry us."

Her laughter rang out. "Oh my God. Can we?"

"We sure can." We got in the car, and the driver knew exactly where to take us. It was late, but the driver assured us that the chapel was open. I sat holding her tiny hand in mine, my heart racing in my chest. I couldn't help but wonder if she was nervous. I was more excited. She was incredible, talented, smart, and so fucking beautiful it hurt. There was nothing fake about her. She was just so natural. She let go of my hand and took a compact out of her bag to check to see if her makeup was still on. "You look beautiful."

When her head turned, her dimples were deep in her cheeks as she smiled at me. "Thank you." The car slowed, and we both looked out the front window. She giggled. "Look how cute it is. Do you think we should have called ahead?"

"It doesn't look like there are many cars. Let's just go in and see."

I got out of the car and reached for her hand. We walked in, and the place was empty. Gwyn hit the little bell on the table a few times. A man dressed like Elvis came out. "Can I help you?"

"I was wondering if you could marry us," I said with a stupid ass grin on my face. I was getting married to a woman I'd known for five days, and I didn't have one bad feeling. I must have lost my mind somewhere.

"I have a wedding in twenty minutes."

"We just want something quick. We have a plane to catch. Nothing fancy." Gwyn smiled at him. I had to stop myself from laughing. It took only a smile from her, and this man was putty in her hands.

"I think I can squeeze in a quick one. Do you have witnesses?"

She looked at me. "Hold on," I said and ran out and got the driver. When we came back in, I said, "We have one."

"Let me get my wife." We watched him walk into a room and then come back out with his wife. We did all the paperwork, and in a matter of five minutes, we were married.

She stood there looking at my hand, at my ring, then at me. Her eyes danced. "You married me," she whispered.

"I did. Now, I get to kiss you whenever I want." I wrapped my hand around her neck and bent down to kiss her. God, she tasted so sweet. "Come on, Mrs. Ashford. Let's go home." We didn't say a word all the way back to the plane. I was a bit worried we might have done the wrong thing. I'd never been so careless in my life. Everything I'd done had been with precision and careful planning. I mean, who bought an engagement ring and let it sit in a safe for eight months? I did. When we got on the plane, I let her sit by the window, and I sat next to her. Still, nothing was said. I kept looking at her, and she had this small smile on her face, making her dimples visible, but it wasn't her usual smile. I only hoped she wasn't thinking twice about us getting married. I squeezed her hand, and she turned her head and smiled at me. But her eyes were unreadable.

Gwyn

I just married a man I'd known for five days. *Holy shit!* If this wasn't the most off the cuff thing I'd done in my life, I didn't know what was. This was crazy shit. My mind wouldn't shut the hell up. I knew why I married him, but was it the smartest thing to do? I looked at him; who the hell wouldn't marry him? He was fucking gorgeous, a huge man. God, he sure knew how to kiss me, and as stupid as it sounded, he had the biggest cock I'd ever seen. Not that I'd seen a lot of them. Only one other, to be correct. But his eyes were so kind, and I couldn't resist. At least, now, Gavin would stay the hell away from me. But that's not the reason I married him. I did it because it felt right. He felt right. I felt it like he did while I was on that stage; he took my breath away. We hadn't said anything since we left the chapel. I figured we both might be in shock. I almost wanted to laugh, but as he squeezed my hand, I could see the worry in his eyes. When the plane leveled out and we were in the air, I looked around the cabin. I could see a few doors in the back of the plane, so I assumed the bedroom was behind one of them. His eyes watched me as I unhooked my seatbelt. He undid his and got up, moving out of my way. Taking a deep breath, I got up and stood in front of him. His fingers ran down my cheek as our eyes locked. Stepping back, I took his hand and headed to the back of the plane.

Opening the middle door, I found the bedroom. When I heard the lock turn on the door, I turned around. "You married me." My voice was quiet.

He smiled. "I did. And you married me."

He leaned back against the door; I suppose waiting for me to talk. "Are you sure?"

He reached out and wrapped his hand around my neck, gently pulling me to him. I went willingly, placing my hands on his massive chest. "I am so very sure," he said on my lips. The kiss I knew was coming, he prolonged. "Angel, talk to me. Tell me what's in your head."

I shook my head. "That's just it. There is nothing in my head. It's just weird for this to feel so right. Is that how you feel?"

"My whole life has been planned out. There hasn't been one thing I've done that wasn't part of the plan. Except for you. But when you looked into my eyes, you touched my soul. It felt like you woke me up, that this is how my life is supposed to go."

Licking my lips, I told him, "I know exactly what you mean. But is this logical?"

He chuckled. "I don't think anything about us is logical, and I think that's what makes it feel so right."

I just stood there, looking at him. My hand reached up to touch his face. "You are so beautiful." He smiled at me, shaking his head. "I want to consummate our marriage so it can't be annulled."

"Do you think they'll try?"

"I don't care." I wanted this man, and I wanted him now.

His hands moved down my body, and he lifted me to his chest. My body was high up against his as he moved to the bed and stood me on it. I let him undress me. He stepped back, looking at my body, his fingers gently touching my bruises. "I'm so sorry this happened to you." Leaning in, he kissed my stomach. "Never again, Angel. Never again."

After pulling his t-shirt over his head, he unbuttoned his jeans, and I felt myself warm even more. My legs were together, and I could feel the wetness pooling between my thighs. "Oh my God," I moaned out when he stood, and his cock stuck straight out from his body. It was so heavy with desire.

His hands turned me around, his lips landing on my ass as he walked me up the bed to the headboard. "Put your hands on the wall." After I did what he asked, he ran his tongue down my spine. "Spread your legs, beautiful." He was so much taller than me that when he knelt behind me, his cock landed between my legs. He didn't push inside but rubbed himself back and forth. The head of his dick rubbed on my bud as his hands and mouth caressed every part of my body he could reach. He was so gentle, so slow in his seduction of my tattered body that I thought I was going to lose my mind. I came two times, so it was a good thing when he slowly pulled me off the wall and held me against his chest. "Tell me if I hurt you," he whispered in my ear, sending chills down my spine.

I felt him at my entrance as he slowly pushed inside of me. "Oh, God," I moaned as my heat sheathed his perfect cock. I could hear his groan vibrating deep inside of him before he let it escape. When I was fully seated on him, I felt so full, so much so that it was painful.

"You okay, Angel?" His mouth was on my neck. I couldn't do anything but nod. "Put your hands on the wall, beautiful." I did as he asked, lifting myself off him a bit, and then he moved, pushing up into me. I wanted to scream; it felt so fucking good.

His hands palmed my nipples, his mouth nipping at every erogenous zone on my neck. "Jaycen, please," I moaned out as he made love to me. So much desire, so much passion I felt for him, from him. He didn't stop moving. I came two more times with him inside of me.

"One more, Angel. Give me one more," he growled, his hand moving down to where we were joined.

"No, I can't. Please, Jaycen." I was afraid I'd pass out if he forced another orgasm out of me. But he didn't stop. His fingers found my bud, and he flattened them and applied the perfect amount of pressure, slowly moving them in a small circle.

"I feel you, beautiful. I feel you tightening. Take me over the edge with you." His words were more than enough to make me orgasm. I felt my whole-body shatter as I exploded, coating him with my orgasm. His cock swelled as he released, buried to the hilt inside of me. His teeth sank into my neck, and his arms wrapped all the way around me as he pulled me to his chest. My head fell back onto his shoulder. He held me like that until my body settled down and completely relaxed against him. "You are now and forever my wife. No one can undo this except for you." Turning my head with his hand, he kissed me. He finally started to soften inside of me, and we separated. Lying down, he pulled me into his embrace and continued kissing me. No other words were said as we both fell asleep.

Jaycen

Gwyn was exquisite, and I couldn't believe she was now my wife. Never had I felt like this while making love to a woman. Making love to her was a mind-altering, life-changing experience. How anyone could hurt someone like her was beyond me. What we just shared was something I'd never experienced. Now, she slept in my arms, where I knew she was safe, where I knew she was loved. Love? Yes, I loved this woman. Rolling over, I pulled her to my chest, wrapping my leg around her. The way my heart jumped when she moved her arm around my waist made me understand how much she meant to me, how much her touch meant to me. Six days, and I was married and in love with my wife. I'd never been the type of person to believe in love at first sight because it sounded like a fairy tale. Somehow, we were connected deep in our souls. My eyes closed as I breathed in her scent, our scent.

When the pilot announced our descent into Chicago, I felt her pulled back. My eyes opened to see her beautiful face looking at me, and she brought her hand up to touch my lips. "Hi, husband."

God, it felt so right to hear her say that to me. My mouth covered hers as my body slipped down the mattress until we were face to face. "Mmm, hi, wife. We should get dressed. We're home."

She just giggled. "I joined the mile-high club."

I laughed. "Me too!"

We got dressed and headed to our seats. Less than an hour later, we were walking into the hotel room, exhausted. I watched as she peeled off her clothes and headed to the room I was using. I followed her slowly and watched her crawl up the bed. Pulling the covers down, she got in and laid on her side with her leg up. She smiled at me. "You coming, or are you going to stand there watching me?"

"I am finding that watching you is something I most definitely enjoy." I dropped my clothes and got in bed behind her, wrapping her in my arms. "Goodnight, Angel."

"Goodnight. I set my alarm. I have so much to do tomorrow."

"Me too. Hey, you want to go look at apartments?"

She snuggled her body closer to mine as I wrapped myself around her. "After this weekend. I've got that huge family thing."

I kissed her shoulder, smiling. I couldn't believe she'd married me. Life was good.

CHAPTER TEN

GWYN

So many emotions, so many thoughts flitted around in my mind about what we'd done the night before. I could feel him wrapped around me, so I opened my eyes. We hadn't moved all night. I didn't want to move then either, but I knew the alarm would be going off soon. He was so warm and so comfortable, and he was my husband. I looked at my hand, at my ring, a small band with tiny diamonds in it, exactly what I'd wanted. It was nothing like the huge ring Gavin had given me; I'd hated that ring. It weighed my hand down, and besides, when he started hitting me, it meant nothing. I took it off every chance I got.

Leaning back, I reached for my phone to shut off the alarm, just as his mouth wrapped around my nipple. Fuck if he didn't get a rise out of me. My hand dropped the phone as my body betrayed me. I could feel his cock on my leg, and I wanted him.

He rolled, pulling me on top of him, kissing me. We didn't need to talk; my core landed right over his cock, my hips rocking already from the sweet way he sucked my nipple. As I moved up his body to find his crown, I soaked his beautiful velvety steel cock with my juices, pressing him inside of me. The moan that escaped us both as I filled myself with him was so erotic that I came instantly. My nipples puckered to a painful point. Pushing up, I walked my hands down his chest, pushing him deeper. Like last night on the plane, he hit my cervix when I seated myself on him.

His hands wrapped around my hips, nearly touching both my stomach and ass. I felt him press, and I started the slow, torturous rhythm of movement, my bud rubbing on his pubic bone. It didn't take but a few minutes before my body started to convulse as my orgasm ripped through me. With my head back, the moan that came from deep inside of me was foreign to me. I had never made such a guttural sound before.

He lay watching me, and when I laid down on his chest, he slowly rolled us onto our sides, his hand pulling my thigh over his, and he made love to me until he swelled and filled me. Our kiss was so intense, our bodies so in tune. This man felt like he had been created just for me.

"Good morning, wife," he whispered on my lips as he kissed me again.

"Mmm, good morning, husband." I touched his lips. "What are you going to do today?"

He kissed my fingers. "Work. I've been neglectful over the past six days. But now that my life is complete, and all my dreams have come true, I think it's time I get my workplace in order."

I couldn't help but giggle. "So, your life is complete? As opposed to the chaotic mess it was just before you saved me?"

"Well, it wasn't that bad. I was just angry and hurt. In a bad mood for like three months."

"And now, is your bad mood gone?"

His hand cupped my breast, and his fingers gently pinched my nipple, causing me to arch my back and moan. "So gone." His mouth came down on mine. God, this man's kisses made me forget my name. My alarm went off, but he didn't stop kissing me. I felt him getting hard. Then his alarm went off, and we chuckled together.

He pulled off me and rolled to shut his off, and I leaned over the bed to grab mine off the floor. As I was turning it off, his hands gripped my hips, pulling me up on my knees. I didn't have time to put the phone down before he was pushing into me from behind. The phone fell to the floor. "Oh, God," I moaned out. He felt so good at this angle.

"I can see my come on myself," he moaned as he pulled out of me. He worked himself in and out for a few minutes, his hips jerking as he hit my end. By the time he finished with me, his thrusts were coming harder and harder, pulling orgasm after orgasm from me. We both collapsed on the bed, and he pulled me on top of him, his mouth covering mine in one of his mind-altering kisses. We both closed our eyes and fell back asleep.

Jaycen

Oh, holy hell, this woman was perfect in every way. Laying here, sexually spent, with her perfect little body wrapped around me, what more could a man ask for? I hadn't a clue. My eyes closed from sheer exhaustion; my body depleted from too many orgasms. I almost laughed, feeling the burn in my body. I wanted more of her; she was my drug. When I opened them again, I lifted my head and chuckled, which woke her.

"Is this what our life is going to be like?" she cooed.

Rolling over, I kissed her. She is so sweet tasting. "I certainly hope so. It's nine-thirty. I think we are late."

She busted out in giggles, pushing on my chest. "I had an appointment at ten. I am in so much trouble." She was moving fast. First to the bathroom, then grabbing her clothes. "Shit, I had this on yesterday when my sister came over. Fuck. Oh well." She giggled. I just laid on the bed watching her. When she was dressed, she crawled up the bed, kissing me. "I have to go. I have the key to the room, and I now know which elevator to take. I'm not sure when I'll be back. It might be late."

I rolled her over to kiss her properly. "I have plans this evening that I can't get out of. I might be late as well."

She lifted her eyebrow at me. "Do these plans include women?"

I had to laugh. "As a matter of fact, they do, but don't worry about me. I'm a married man." I held up my hand.

"You're fucking right, you are." Her hand was on my face, her eyes suddenly serious. "What we did last night was crazy. Jaycen…"

I didn't let her finish. "Never, beautiful. I am not that kind of man. Besides, if I did, I would never get to do this again." I kissed her. "I like this, so very much."

"Yeah?"

"Oh yeah. Now, go, before I make love to you again."

"When I heal, and the bruises are gone, will you fuck me?"

I didn't mean to growl, but I did. "Oh, you can bet this perfect ass of yours that I'm going to fuck you." I couldn't stop myself. I had to kiss her; I had to touch her. We got lost in one another again. God, she was heaven. I hated to let her leave, but I needed to get to the office. Tonight was Caden's big night. I wasn't sure I could sit back and watch him fuck multiple women right before he got married, but it was his night. If that's what he wanted to do, then who was I to say a word to him? He'd always been that way. Still couldn't figure out why he was getting married. I mean, Ally was beautiful and such a sweet woman.

I jumped in the shower, then left and headed to the office.

Gwyn

I couldn't get the damn smile off my face. Three times in one morning. I mean, Jesus, he was some kind of machine, and he was all mine. I didn't even bother going home. Jumping in a cab, I headed to the bridal shop. I was late but not that late. I wanted to get up early so I could go home and shower and pack some things. But, oh well. Pulling up, I could see my mother, grandmother, sister, and her friend Ariel. When I walked in, all eyes were on me. I hated it. The questions were going to come at me left and right, and this day was supposed to be about my sister, not me.

She came rushing up to me, her voice low. "Did you marry someone?"

I laughed. "This isn't about me today. It's about you. We'll talk later tonight. Let's get your dress perfect." I looked at her face, whispering, "You did a good job. I can't even see the bruise."

"I'm getting better at covering them up."

"Please, reconsider."

"It's fine. He apologized, bought me flowers, begged for my forgiveness, and gave me this." She held her hand out, and on her wrist was a diamond bracelet.

I just smiled and shook my head. "It's not worth it."

I took her hand and walked into the shop. We spent hours there, getting fitted. She looked so beautiful in her dress. My mom didn't say much to me, but her eyes didn't leave my face or my body when I changed to get in my dress. While we sat there waiting for my sister, she reached over and took my hand. Her thumb ran across the ring Jaycen had given me. Her words were soft as she told me, "I'm so glad you got out. I hope he's a good man."

My throat closed, and I had to seriously fight back the tears. "He is, Mom. He is." She squeezed my hand and didn't say another word to me.

After the bridal shop, we all went out to lunch, which I was grateful for because I was starving. We had a good time talking and laughing. As we were leaving, my mom, grandma, and Ariel were getting into the car, while my sister and I were waiting for a cab. My mom lived outside of the city, and we lived in the city. "So, tell me, Gwyn. This ring on your finger says you got married. Did you really? Gavin told Caden that some guy punched him in the head and told him not to touch you again, that he was your husband."

I took a deep breath, but before I could say a word, Gavin walked up, grabbed me by the arm, and pulled me away from the street. "Tell me you didn't marry that guy. You are mine." He shoved me so hard against the wall.

My initial reaction was to knee him in the balls. When he bent over, I leaned into him. "I do not belong to you. What I do in my life is none of your fucking business. Go talk to my father, Gavin. If you touch me again, I will fucking ruin you." I shoved him, and he fell to the sidewalk. As I walked away, he grabbed my leg, and I swung my bag at him. He let go of me, and I continued back to my sister. A cab pulled up as he was getting up, and we got in and drove away.

"What the hell are you doing, Gwyn?"

"Fighting back. I'm not going to live like that. I refuse. I am so much more than a man who hurts me."

"And what, this new guy isn't like that?"

I just looked at her. "What makes you think there is a new guy? Why can't I just be fighting for myself, for who I am? You know what? You really need to get a fucking backbone, because he is going to kill you eventually." Reaching in my purse, I grabbed twenty dollars and shoved it in the slot, then told the cab driver, "Please, pull over here. I'll walk."

Jaycen

Walking into the office felt weird. I got my messages from Heidi as I headed into my office. The first call to return was to Hartman records.

"Hey, Steve, it's Jaycen Ashford."

"I got the paperwork back. It's all signed, and the check should be delivered to you this afternoon. So, how do you want to do this?"

"It's all yours. I signed a new group called The Vibe. These guys are good, so treat them well. I will inform everyone, and you can take over on Monday. I'm going to need a few days to get everything done. Thanks, Steve."

"Thank you, but I have to ask, why did you finally agree to sell?"

I laughed. "I think I'm done. I want more and selling out to you has afforded me a good life."

"This isn't because of Ashley, is it? That broad was never good enough for you."

"You're right, she wasn't. But yes and no. If I have a chance in hell of having a decent relationship, I think being home once in a while is a good place to start. Listen, I need to go. I've got some news to explain."

"When can I go public with this?"

Chuckling, I told him, "Friday will be fine. I just need a few days. Otherwise, I'm done."

"You got it. Good luck, Jay. I hope you get everything you want in life."

"Thanks, Steve. I'll see you around."

I disconnected the call as my buzzer rang. "Mr. Ashford, there is a messenger here to see you."

"Send him in, Heidi, and then, when he leaves, can you come in here please?"

"Certainly, sir."

The door opened, and a man walked in and handed me an envelope. I thanked him and opened the envelope. It felt weird holding a check for two-hundred and fifty million dollars. My life's work had a price tag. I should have felt something, remorse or defeat, but looking at my left hand, I didn't feel anything but happiness. I wanted to talk to her, to see her. I slipped the check in my pocket just as Heidi came in.

This was going to be difficult; she'd been with me from the beginning. "Please, have a seat." She sat in a chair across from me with her notepad and a smile on her face. "This is difficult for me," I started. "You've been with me from the start, but keep in mind that your job here is secure. I've sold the company to Hartman Records." She sat there and looked at me, her eyes wide. "They are taking possession on Monday. I have a bonus check for you for all the years of service you've given me."

Her head drooped, and she didn't say anything for a long time. When she picked her head up, she had tears falling on her rosy cheeks. "I don't know what to say." Her voice was soft. "Can I ask why?"

I smiled. "Many reasons. I think I'm just burnt out."

She smiled. "Would it have anything to do with that ring on your finger?"

Picking up my hand, I looked at it and laughed. "Not at first, but yeah."

"Please, tell me you didn't marry that horrible Ashley."

I laughed loudly. "Oh, no, that was never going to work out. I married a beautiful, talented photographer. She sort of caught me by surprise. I think it was love at first sight, to be honest with you."

"Well, I'm sad that it's over, but I'm happy for you. I was worried you were going to work yourself to death."

"Thank you." I reached across my desk and grabbed the envelope I'd prepared for her, handing it to her. "Thank you, Heidi, for so many years of service. I hope everything goes well for you."

She took the envelope and then hugged me. I watched her walk out then took a few deep breaths before moving back around my desk. The sun reflected off my ring, and my heart actually warmed. Just then, my phone rang.

"Jaycen Ashford."

"Hello, Mr. Ashford. This is Mrs. Ashford." She giggled.

My smile hurt my face. "Hello, Angel. How's your day going?"

"You don't want to know."

I sat up straight. "What happened?"

"I ran into Gavin coming out of the restaurant."

"Did he touch you?"

"He grabbed me by the arm and slammed me against the wall, but I kneed him in the balls then hit him a few times with my bag." I could hear the smile on her face.

"Did he hurt you?" I tried not to smile at her enthusiasm for hurting him.

She giggled. "No, but I got into it with my sister over it. They know I am married. He ran and told my sister's fiancé since they are best buds. I suppose abusers stick together. My mom told me she's happy I got out. She asked me if you were a good man."

My heart fluttered. "What did you tell her?" I was fishing for a compliment.

She laughed. "I told her the truth."

"Which is?"

Still laughing, she said, "I told her you were one of the good guys. The best."

"Thank you, I try."

"Jaycen, I'm not sure how my night is going to go, so I'm probably going to be at the hotel early."

"Well, if I know you are waiting for me, then I'm going to have to cut my night short."

"No, don't you dare. I think I just wanted to make sure it was okay that I go there."

My heart sank. "You are my wife. You belong there. Of course, it's fine. Hey."

"Yeah?"

"Meet me there. This is a conversation I need to have with you in person. I'll meet you there in fifteen minutes, okay?"

"Okay."

I disconnected the call as I made it to the elevator. When I walked into the room, she was sitting on the couch. I took off my jacket, laying it over the back of the chair, then reached out for her hands. When she stood, I picked her up, wrapping her legs around me, then sat down in the chair with her on my thighs. Wrapping my fingers around her beautiful neck, I pulled her mouth to mine for a kiss.

"Does that feel like I want you here with me?" She nodded. "I know it's so crazy, what we did, what we feel, in such a short time, but I know it's right. I feel it, beautiful. I feel it right here." I put my hand on my heart. "Stay with me. Move in with me."

Her fingers were on my lips. "Yeah?"

"Yes. I didn't even think to ask you if you wanted to be here with me. Do you?"

Her smile lit up the fucking room. "So much. So much, yes, Jaycen. I can't stop thinking about you. I want to know everything there is to know about you, but it's like I've known you my whole life."

"Whatever happens outside to confuse us, just know that this is what I want. This right here, this is what I want. Come Sunday, there won't be anyone but us. Only we can undo this. You know how much I want this?" She shook her head. I needed to say this the right way. "I didn't ask you to sign a prenup. If I had asked Ashley to marry me, like I'd once planned, she would have had to sign a prenup. I don't think I ever fully trusted her. But for some reason, I trust you. Call me crazy, but I don't believe you are going anywhere. I think you want this as much as I do."

She scooted closer to me. Leaning in, she pressed her lips to mine. "I do, Jaycen. I do." She so sweetly kissed me. I wanted to take her into the bedroom and make love to her, but I had so much shit to do.

"If I didn't have a million things to do today, you would be naked and on that bed. I missed a meeting to come here. You are so important to me, Angel. I don't want you to think or feel anything less."

"Thank you."

She moved to get off my lap, but I pulled her back to me, my hands on her perfect ass. "I'm not done with you yet." I kissed her sweet mouth again.

Pulling back, her smile did me in. Her fucking dimples would be my undoing. "You go, go to work. I'm going to my apartment to pack some clothes. I'll be in that bed waiting for you tonight."

"Promise?"

She nodded and kissed me again. I stood and lowered her down my chest so she could feel my cock, just so she knew how much I wanted her. "I'll see you tonight. Five more days until Sunday."

"Five more days." Her eyes sparkled.

I didn't want to leave. I found it harder and harder to leave her, to be away from her. It had been nearly a week, but it felt like a lifetime. I was excited to get to know her better, to learn everything about her. Putting on my jacket to leave felt wrong. "Can I wake you up when I get home?" I asked as I pulled her to me.

"I hope so. Goodbye, Jaycen. Have a good day at work," she smarted.

I laughed and kissed her hard. Walking out of there was the hardest fucking thing I'd done in a long time. My cock was hard, pressing against my boxers to be free. I buttoned my jacket so it wouldn't be noticeable. Standing at the elevator, I turned to look at the door. "What the fuck?" My feet had me moving back to the hotel room. When I opened the door, she was standing there, ready to leave. I just picked her up and walked into the bedroom. "You are what matters to me. Nothing else. Do you hear me?"

She nodded, and her fingers touched my lips. "I think I love you." Her words came out soft and went directly to my heart.

"That's good, Angel, because I think I love you." I don't know how we ended up naked, but when I pushed into her, every molecule in body collided and exploded. It took only five pumps, and I was gone.

Her giggle filled the room as I lay on her, perching myself up on my elbows. Her hands cupped my face. "Oh my God, what was that?"

I had to laugh; her giggle was infectious. "That was me being a fifteen-year-old. I'm almost embarrassed that it happened so fast."

She was still giggling. "Don't be. It makes me happy to know that I do that to you." I felt myself growing hard again, still inside of her. Her face changed as she felt me fill her. "Oh, Jaycen, please." She lifted her body off the bed to kiss me. My hips moved, pressing into her. My God, the way she made me feel. Never had a woman made me feel so much. The second time around lasted much longer. When we finished, we were both exhausted. "Is this how our life is going to be?"

I chuckled. "I hope so." Pushing up, I pulled from her. "I would rather be here with you than any other place on this planet." I knew then that I'd made the right decision to sell my company. I couldn't wait to explore our life together.

She sat up, climbing onto my thighs. Her kiss was one I didn't know, and we'd shared a great many kisses. "I never believed that I would feel like this about someone. I don't want to leave you to go out there into the world. I want to stay here, right here with you. After this stupid family weekend, and all the bullshit that's leading up to it, I don't have to be near them, the negativity, or the anguish they perpetuate. I am the luckiest girl in the world to have had you see me. To have been in the same space as you that night. Promise me, Jaycen, that what we have is real."

I felt myself choking up. Tears were building in my eyes. I picked up her hand. "This right here," I twirled the ring around her finger, "is my promise, Angel. What we have is so real." My voice was low as a tear fell from my eye and onto my cheek.

She wiped it off with her finger. "I believe you. I trust you. I love you."

My mouth crashed down on hers, my hand wrapped around her neck so she couldn't escape. She gave as good, if not better, than she got. Pulling back, I put my forehead on hers, trying to catch my breath. "I love you, Angel."

She smiled and got off my legs, and I watched as she walked to the bathroom, then I heard the water. I didn't care what the fuck I was supposed to be doing outside this room. I got up and joined her. It was a quick shower to wash the smell of sex off us. We walked out together, holding hands. On the street, we got into the car together, and I dropped her off at her place before I went back to the office to end that chapter of my life.

I got out with her and walked her to her door, giving her a kiss. "I'll see you tonight."

"You bet your ass you will."

She went in, and I left.

Gwyn

I wanted to squeal like a little girl at how happy I was, but he would've thought I was in trouble. Air punching seemed so stupid, but my fist went in the air. I'd hit the jackpot with him. After locking the door, I went to my room and started packing. I needed to make sure I had enough clothes for the next few days.

Then I got my camping gear out and got that all ready. I figured I could take it over a little bit at a time. My phone buzzed, and I grabbed it. Seeing it was my sister, I answered it rather rudely. "What?"

"Gwyn, I'm so sorry. I have no idea what's wrong with me. I think I'm just nervous."

"It doesn't matter. After Saturday, I'm done with this family. I refuse to live my life like you and Mom. I know my worth, and it far exceeds fucking Gavin Highland."

"Can I ask you why you didn't tell me you got married?"

"Because it isn't anyone's business what I do. My life is my own. I am responsible for my own happiness."

"He makes you happy?"

"No. I make me happy. He just enhances that. I'm not discussing this with you or anyone else. I'm sorry if that hurts you, but you go back and tell that fucker who beats you, and then he fucking tells Gavin, then Gavin goes and cries to Dad. You people are all fucked in the head. If you think he is going to stop hurting you, then you are crazy. It will only get worse, and if you feel your own worth isn't worth a fucking thing, then what the hell do you want from me? I can't be here for you, sister. I can't watch while he destroys what little bit is left. I will be there Saturday. I will stand by your side, and I will smile and pretend to be happy for you because you are my sister, and I love you more than anything else. Please, just don't ask me to be a part of your everyday life."

I heard her sniffle. "I don't know how to be strong enough to walk away."

"How about taking a long hard look in the mirror? Are you worth more than those bruises?"

"Yes."

"Then find it within yourself. I can't tell you how. It has to come from within you. Listen, I'm not sure I can make it to dinner tonight. I've had enough of fucking Gavin Highland for the rest of my life. I'm tired of being stalked and followed by his fucking goons. I just want my life."

"I understand. Do you want to just have a night in? I can come over, and we can have some wine and watch a movie or something."

"No, I'm just going to do some packing."

"Are you moving in with him?"

I wasn't going to answer her. I was so tired of her telling everyone my business. "Listen, I need to go. I will see you Saturday. I love you."

"Okay. I love you, too."

I disconnected the call. "What the fuck?" I huffed, looking at my phone. She was on a fact-finding mission for fucking Gavin. I finished with all the shit I wanted to do, then I went to the fridge and grabbed a few things, putting them in my backpack, and headed out. If I never slept in that apartment again for the rest of my life, I'd be a happy girl. It was time for me to live my life the way I wanted, with whom I wanted, and none of them were going to say shit about it.

Jaycen

Walking back into the office, which wasn't going to be my office anymore, felt right. Making love to her felt right. Everything about it felt right. I walked into the conference room, which was filled with my staff, and the looks on their faces made me chuckle.

"I'm sorry I'm late, considering I called this meeting." They all nodded. I didn't want to sit; I felt too energized to sit. She made me feel so full of energy. "I asked you all here to let you know what is going on. I signed a new group, The Vibe, and I sold the company." All of their heads turned to look at me. "Don't worry, everyone's jobs are secure. It was part of the deal."

"Sir, can I ask why?"

I laughed. "I just think I'm finished." It was the only thing I could think of to say. It was the only thing I wanted to say. "Friday is my last day, and Hartman Records is taking over on Monday. I have bonus checks for each of you, so check in with Heidi before you leave. Thank you all for everything you have done. I appreciate it." I smiled and walked out.

My phone buzzed in my pocket. "Yeah?"

"What the fuck, asshole? Where the hell have you been?"

I laughed. "In another world."

"Well, get your ass back here. I'm getting married in three days. You ready to party?"

I looked at my hand, at my ring. I didn't know how to tell him I'd gotten married without him. "Yeah, what time and where?"

"Me and you, bud. We're going to Maxi's, of course."

"Really, a sex club? Aren't we more mature than that?"

"I'm not. I want to fuck until I can't move. Hey, you could use a good fuck. What's it been, three months?"

"I prefer my woman to be unique, not used up."

"What the fuck? You used to love that place."

"Yeah, when I was in my twenties, when I didn't know any better, and we were fucking hornier than a dog in heat."

He laughed. "I got two boxes of condoms just for the occasion."

I rolled my eyes. "Man, I'm not sure this is what I want to do. I'm sorry. Why don't you take your brother? I'm sure he could use a night in bed with some hot women. Maybe we can get dinner tomorrow night or something. I'm really not in the mood to go to a sex club."

"I can't tomorrow. I've got dinner with Ally's family, and Friday, I have a dinner meeting with Klamco. I want that fucking company, and this bastard is digging in."

"Sorry to hear that. Listen, we'll get together when you get back from your honeymoon. I'm not in the mood to do this tonight. I've got some shit going on here, and I think it should be my priority."

"I hear you, man. Sometimes, I think owning my own company is a bigger pain in my ass than it would be to just work for me."

I busted out laughing. "You're an asshole for a boss. You would more than likely punch yourself in the face."

He laughed. "No doubt. All right, man, your loss if you're not going, but I get it. You're going to be there Saturday, right?"

"Fuck yeah. You're my best friend. I wouldn't miss watching you get married for anything."

"Thanks, I'll see you Saturday morning at ten a.m."

"See ya, and, Caden, rethink the sex club."

"Fuck that shit. I'm fucking all night long. I think I'm going to break my old record. What was it, ten orgasms in a night?"

Shaking my head, I laughed. "Something like that. Don't break your dick, asshole."

"Not a chance of that happening. I'll see you Saturday."

"Yep."

When I set my phone down, I felt sick for Ally. She was such a sweetheart and didn't deserve this shit. No woman should have to put up with that. I just didn't understand how you could say you love someone and then cheat.

Pushing it all out of my head, I got to work. Five hours later, I was done. Heading out, I went back to the hotel. I wasn't expecting to find Gwyn naked and in bed. She was sleeping, and God, she was beautiful. I took off my clothes and crawled in the bed, pulling her to me.

It was undeniable to me the way she felt next to me. She rolled over, her hand coming to rest on my face. I watched as her beautiful eyes opened. "What are you doing here?"

I smiled. "What are you doing here?"

"I asked you first."

"Well, I blew off my plans. I didn't want to hang out with my buddy tonight."

"Why not?"

"Because I have no desire to go to a sex club."

She started laughing. "Please, tell me there really aren't sex clubs."

"Oh, there are. What are you doing here?"

"I got into a fight with my sister. She called me, as always, to get information for fucking Gavin about you. I'm just tired of all the deception. Gavin and her fiancé have ruined our relationship. I walked away from an abusive relationship, and I am so tired of listening to her whine and cry every time he fucking beats her up. So, I packed some stuff and came here to wait for you. I guess I was tired, so here we are." She paused. "Really?"

I laughed, kissing her. "Really. Don't worry, Angel. I wasn't going. I'm starving. How about you?"

"I'm always hungry. Really? A sex club?"

I laughed, rolling over to grab the phone. "Really. Why, do you want to go? We can go watch if you want." I sat up, and she flung herself onto my back, biting my shoulder.

"Not tonight, but as long as we don't have to participate, I'm game," she whispered in my hear. Her words went straight to my cock. She climbed around to sit on me. "All this talk of sex," was all she got out of her mouth before I kissed her. Holding her in my arms as she lifted herself onto my cock was so erotic. With her feet planted on the bed, she took me time and time again. I watched her look down at our connection. "Look, baby," she moaned.

My eyes moved to where hers were locked. "Jesus, Angel. I'm going to fucking come."

"Please, Jaycen. Please." Her eyes bore into mine. My hand moved on its own to gently touch her hood. Her arms pushed on my shoulders as her body leaned back to convulse. God, she was magnificent. I put my hands on her hips and brought myself home. When she picked her head up, her eyes glowed, and her lip was tucked between her teeth.

"So, fucking beautiful," I growled as I wrapped my arms around her, kissing her like I was walking through the valley of death, and she was the last breath I would ever take. When I finished, I stood, and her legs wrapped around my waist, her hands moving to my face. I walked us to the shower and leaned her against the wall. My hands were in her hair. I wanted to pull it tight, but she was still sore, so I kissed her again. "Let's get you cleaned up and have some dinner."

Our shower was quick. While she dried off, I ordered food then went to grab some pajama bottoms. Her clothes were hanging on hangers next to mine. I opened a few of the drawers and found her panties and bras were in one. I couldn't stop smiling. I was married, and my wife was moving in.

Gwyn

I felt like I was floating on a cloud, but eventually, I would have to float back to earth and face the assholes in my life. I was moving my hair around on my head to see what the gashes looked like when Jaycen came in. "What are you doing?" He laughed.

"Trying to see how my head is healing. Will you look?"

He came up behind me and shifted my hair around. "They look good, still red, and a few are scabbing over." I watched him in the mirror; he was beautiful. "I ordered some fish. I hope you like fish."

I smiled. "I'll eat pretty much anything." I moved away from him and went to get dressed. He was in the living room on the couch when I came out. "I'm having dinner with my grandmother tomorrow, so I won't be back until around nine."

"Not a problem. I've got some things to do. I need to find us a place to live. You game to go hunting with me?"

"Sure. I would suggest we stay at my place, but I had sex with Gavin in my bed. I want to burn it."

"Well, we can buy all new furniture, and get a very big bed."

"I like the bed here, and those sheets. My God, I've never felt anything so comfortable before." I crawled onto the couch next to him, and he pulled me to his chest.

"I'll ask what kind of bed and sheets, and we can get them."

"Do you plan on spoiling me?"

"Every damn day for the rest of your life if you'll let me."

I laughed. "Will you let me do the same for you?"

"Of course."

"Then you have a deal." We snuggled together, waiting for the food to come. My eyes closed longer and longer each time I blinked. I was so tired.

"Angel," he said, softly shaking me. "The food's here."

Sitting up, I smiled at him. "I'm tired. Can we go to bed after we eat?"

"We can do anything you want. I'm tired, too, so let's eat."

He opened the door and took the tray from the guy. We sat on the couch and devoured everything he'd ordered. Once we finished, he stood, reached for my hand, and led me into the bedroom. There, he slowly undressed me, then picked me up and laid me down on the bed.

"I do know how to walk and undress myself." I giggled.

"I know, but I want to take care of you, so just be quiet and enjoy it." He dropped his bottoms and pulled his t-shirt off, then crawled in behind me. The light went off, and his warmth encased my body. His arms held me safely in his embrace. When he kissed my head, I felt his body relax. "Goodnight, Angel."

"Mmm, goodnight, Jaycen." That's all I remember until the alarm went off on his phone.

Jaycen

Waking up with her in my arms seemed to be my favorite thing lately. We hadn't moved all night. Quietly, I got out of bed. I wanted her again. I wanted to make love to her, but I knew she had to be exhausted. Hell, we went to bed at eight-thirty last night, and neither of us moved. When I got out of the shower, she was in the same position I'd left her in. Standing there looking at her, my cock hardened. She was so fucking spectacular it hurt. I still couldn't believe she was my wife, that she'd married me. Her bruises were starting to fade, yellowing her beautiful body. Soon they'd be gone, and I could watch her skin pink when I bit her. I ran my hand through my wet hair, my cock thickening even more at the thought of taking her to a sex club. I wondered how Caden made out. Fucking asshole. I moved to the closet to get dressed. One more day, and I wouldn't ever have to set a fucking alarm again.

Her hand touched my back, and all thoughts left my mind. Her lips gently kissed my spine. She didn't say a word as I slowly turned. Her hand landed on my stomach, while her other hand wrapped around my thick cock. "Mmm," she moaned as she lowered her body to the floor.

When her warm, sweet mouth wrapped around my crown, I was

in heaven. It only took her a few pushes before I felt her throat open like a fucking python as she swallowed me whole. Her lips wrapped around my base, and she fucking swallowed. I couldn't stop it; there was no way. I was at her mercy as she milked me of every ounce of cum I had. It was so intense my legs started to shake. When she finished, she stood up and kissed my stomach. Looking up into my eyes, she smiled. Then she turned around and walked out of the closet. I watched her go, her perfect ass my view. Stepping forward, I watched her walk into the bathroom, then I heard the shower turn on. Chuckling, I got dressed. Never, in the three years I was with Ashley, did anything like that happen. But Gwyn wasn't Ashley. They weren't even on the same level. I made a mental note to never compare them again.

With my tie and jacket in my hand, I headed out to the living area to order breakfast. I was going through my messages when my phone buzzed, and Caden's picture flashed on the screen. "What the fuck, asshole? Did you fuck your dick off or what?"

He was laughing. "Man, did you miss a good time."

Thinking about last night, I thought I'd probably had a better time. "Did you use both boxes of condoms?"

"Oh, fuck yeah. I just walked in the door. Ally is pissed off. She said I smelled like sex." He laughed. "Probably because that's all I did for ten hours. Anyway, I set her straight. My body doesn't belong to her until after I put a ring on her finger."

"You are such an asshole. I don't know how she puts up with you."

He was still laughing. "Because I know how to fuck her."

Chuckling, I shook my head. "Try making love to her."

He guffawed out. "Who has time for that shit? My dick gets hard, I want a release. Making love is for pussies."

"Then, I'm the biggest pussy you know."

"Oh, so you're fucking this Angel girl?"

"Nope, haven't fucked her yet, but I'm hopeful."

"Oh, please don't tell me you're making love to her. You are such a pussy."

"Every chance I get. Hey, listen, my food is here, and I have a busy day today. I'm glad you made it out alive. Did your brother have a good time?"

"No, I took Ally's sister's fiancé; he pulled the poor me card. Her sister's been out of town for work, so he needed some."

"You guys are pigs. Talk soon, man."

"Later, Jay."

I disconnected the call just as room service knocked on the door. Gwyn was still in the bathroom. I knocked on the door. "Angel, breakfast is here."

She opened the door with a smile on her face. "Why do you call me Angel?"

My hand wrapped around her neck. "Because you have a voice like an Angel."

Her whole face lit up when she smiled. "Thank you."

I had to kiss her. She tasted like peppermint. "Come on. Let's eat. I've got today and tomorrow until my vacation starts, and I'm looking forward to spending the time alone with you."

She giggled all the way into the living area. We sat and ate, both of us just smiling at each other. "Thank you for the closet."

She busted out laughing. "No, thank you. I needed the protein. So, how did your friend do at the sex club?"

I nearly choked on my coffee. "Apparently, very well. He was there all night."

"So, later in this relationship, will you take me there?"

Looking at her, I could see she was serious and curious at the same time. "I'm not sure I would feel comfortable letting you watch other men fucking women."

The laughter that rang through the room made my heart burst. "Baby, I'm pretty sure I could handle it. I would be worried that you would get off on it."

"If I'm being honest, I'm sure I would, but not for the reasons you are thinking. It wouldn't be because of something someone else was doing; it would be because I might see something that I could see us doing."

She set her glass of orange juice down and got up, then climbed on my lap. "Are there things you want to do to me, Jaycen, that are out of the norm?" Her voice was laden with desire.

"Oh, Angel, so many things." My hands rested on her perfect ass.

"Would you want to tie me up?"

"Perhaps."

"Would you want to blindfold me?"

"Perhaps."

"Do you want to spank me, Jaycen?" Her voice purred, and her hips rocked gently. She was getting riled up. I was learning her body, and it was such a turn on.

"I'd like to bite you all over this perfect ass of yours." She was getting me excited.

"I want to go to this sex club, Jaycen. I want you to take me. I want to watch and learn. I want you to show me things you'd like to do with me, or to me."

"Angel, I will give you anything you desire."

She leaned forward; her breath hot on my face. "When my body heals, husband, I want you to fuck me. I want to feel your huge cock slamming into me. Will you give me that?"

I was so fucking hard. My hands moved up her sides, pulling her shirt off. I unhooked her bra and cupped her fantastic tits in my hands, pinching her nipples between my thumbs and fingers. Her moans nearly drove me to abandon my day and fuck her all day long. When her hand moved down my chest to rub my cock under my slacks, that was it for me. I had to have her. As she looked deep into my eyes. "You okay?" she whispered as she drew my bottom lip into her mouth.

I wanted to say something incredible, but no words came to my brain. So, I just smiled at her and nodded. It was all I could do. When I picked my head up, I felt a tear fall on my cheek. My emotions spun like a full tornado in my mind. I reached up to touch her beautiful face. Her bruises were nearly gone. My fingers wrapping around her neck, I kissed her. My life had been changed, altered in its course of direction by this beautiful woman in front of me. She was mine, designed for me, as I was for her. She would never know anything less than all of me. "You…" It seemed so insignificant to try to put my feelings into words. "I…" Her smile did me in. I had nothing.

"I know." She kissed me sweetly. "I know, Jaycen. I feel it, too."

I nodded, dropping my head to her chest. The emotions that raged through me were so foreign, so powerful that I couldn't hold back the tears. Her hands wrapped around me, pulling me into her embrace.

Gwyn

When I held him, it felt like we were one. I'd found him, the man who was put on this earth for me. I never believed in this stuff, old souls loving for eternity, that even in death, their love never dies. I loved him. Crazy, stupid love. Six days, and I was in love. I could feel his tears on my chest. His love for me was all too clear and plain to see. We were so connected, no one would or could ever understand. Slowly, he calmed down and lifted his head. I wiped his tears off his cheeks with my thumbs.

"Come on, beautiful. Let's get you cleaned up." He pushed up, taking his slacks all the way off. He was always so concerned for me. I'd never had that, and I wondered if he had. He picked me up, setting me high on his chest. My hands were on his face as he stepped out of his slacks and carried us to the shower.

We didn't talk. He just touched my face with the softest eyes and the sweetest smile. He changed into a different suit and cleaned up the mess we made while I got dressed. "You ready?" I smiled at him.

We walked out of the hotel holding hands and climbed into his car. "Where can I drop you?"

"My apartment. I need to grab my stuff for Sunday and my dress for dinner tonight."

"Did you want me to go with you?"

"No, it's with my grandmother, so Gavin and my father won't be a problem. She's my father's mother, so they'll be on their best behavior. I'll walk her out and grab a cab. I shouldn't be too late, maybe ten."

He squeezed my hand. "I'm looking forward to Sunday."

"Me too. I'm looking forward to telling the world that you're my husband."

He leaned over and kissed my temple. "I'm looking forward to a great many things, Angel."

When we pulled up to my building, I climbed onto his lap and held his face. "Will you tell me tonight what was going on this morning?"

He smiled. "I'll try. Come on, I'll walk you up."

At my door, he embraced me in his hold. "You've become the most important thing in my life. Please, be safe, beautiful."

"I will. I promise. Will you be back before I leave?"

"I hope to be. What time is dinner?"

"Seven."

"I'll make sure I'm there by six." He kissed me sweetly. "Goodbye, Angel."

I smiled. "Goodbye, Jaycen."

He waited until I shut the door.

CHAPTER ELEVEN

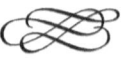

JAYCEN

After she shut the door, I stood there, feeling a void in my heart. I didn't want to be without her. I didn't want to leave her alone, not while the world was still in the dark about us. He needed to understand that she was no longer his, that she belonged to me.

Walking to the elevator, I realized that she was a very strong woman, and I needed to trust in that. I couldn't suffocate her or try to control everything that happened in her life. Smiling, I couldn't help but think that I was married to a strong, independent woman. Something new for me. Ashley wasn't like that; she was a leech compared to Gwyn.

When I got in the car, I happened to turn to look at her building when I saw that fucker walk in the door. My blood boiled in my veins as I opened the door. "Call the police," I said to my driver, then I was moving. The elevator doors closed, which meant I had to wait or take the stairs. I would be winded by the time I got there if I ran up that many flights, so I waited.

I ran off the elevator just as he was pushing his way into her apartment. I could hear him yelling at her. "This isn't going to go well for you if you keep fighting me. You are mine." I was halfway there when the door flew open, and I heard a sickening thud. I knew it was her body being slammed between the door and the wall. Then he slammed the door shut. I could hear her screaming, "Get the fuck out!"

When I got to the door, I heard him hit her. "Not on your fucking life. You are mine!" he screamed. My foot kicked the door, and it flew open. He had her by the hair, his hand pulled back into a fist. The look on his face said it all. The fear made me smile. He let her go, and when she fell to the floor, he stepped back into the room.

"You want to hit someone, fucker, let's go." I stepped forward, swinging, connecting with his jaw. Just like the boxer that day in the ring, his feet left the floor, and he was on his back, out like a light.

I turned and knelt in front of her. She had her head down. "Angel?" She shook her head. I reached and lifted her face. She had blood pouring from her eye and her mouth. "Come on. I've got you." I picked her up and sat her on the counter in the kitchen, then grabbed the towel on the counter and got it wet. She didn't say a word, but I could feel her body trembling. I wrung the towel out before pressing it against her eye. Her body flinched away from my touch. "No, beautiful, don't do that," I whispered to her. That's when she broke. Her sobs started slow then came harder as I embraced her. My eyes stayed glued to the fucker lying on the floor. When the police came, I left her sitting on the counter. "I want to press charges against this man. He attacked my wife. He tried to rape her."

"Sir, who is your wife?"

She came out of the kitchen. "I am."

"Oh my god, Gwyn." One of the female officers walked up to her. "Seriously?" She looked shocked.

"I want him arrested; this is the third time in a week..."

"Fourth, well, fifth actually," she corrected me.

"That he attacked her."

An ambulance was called, and the paramedics came in and woke him up. He was arrested and taken to the hospital. "I'll come down to the station after I get cleaned up," Gwyn told the woman.

"I'm sorry about this. Your father isn't going to be happy about this."

I watched Gwyn; I watched the blank look in her eyes. She just shook her head. "Thanks for coming."

When they all left, she just stood there. When I moved, she flinched. "Hey." She slowly lifted her head. "I love you." It was the only thing I could say. She gave me a small smile, one that didn't include her dimples. "Let me take you back to the hotel."

She nodded. "I need to get my dress for dinner." I watched her walk into her bedroom. She came out with a few bags and her dress. "I need to take this stuff with me. It's the only stuff here that matters to me. The rest I don't care about. I'm not coming back here."

I called my driver and asked him to come up and help us. All in all, she had five bags, her camping gear, and her dress. After we got back to the hotel, I closed the door to the room, and she dropped her things and screamed. I pulled off my jacket and pulled her into my arms before she could finish. "I've got you," I whispered. She collapsed in my arms. Picking her up, I carried her to bed. Kicking off my shoes, I laid down with her in my arms, holding her while she cried. Eventually, she fell asleep. I managed to get my phone out of my pocket and sent a text to Heidi. I told her I wouldn't be back in the office asked if she would please pack up my personal items and send them to the hotel. Then I texted Hartman.

~The company is yours. I'm done. Take it now. Thanks for everything. ~

~You sure? Hope all is well. ~

~Positive. ~

I dropped my phone and wrapped myself around her. This was what mattered; she was what mattered to me. Never again was I going to leave her alone, not until that fucker understood she was not his. She was mine.

Hours later, when she moved, I opened my eyes. Her lip was swollen and had a cut on it, and her eye was puffy. "I'm so sorry," she whispered.

"Don't ever apologize for that fucker. I'm the one who is sorry. I shouldn't have left you. It'll never happen again, not until he is either in jail or fucking dead. You are all that matters to me."

She sat up. "Oh, my head hurts." Looking at me, her hand touched my chest. "I ruined your shirt."

I looked down and noticed it had blood all over it. "It's just a shirt. Do you want me to call Alex? That cut on your eye looks like it might need some stitches."

"Probably. Don't you have to be at work?"

I chuckled. "I no longer have a job."

"You quit? How the hell are you going to take care of me?" she smarted with a small smile on her lips.

I laughed. "Well, with this." I pulled out my wallet, handing her the check.

"Jaycen, what the hell? This is a check for two hundred and fifty million dollars. Is this real?"

I laughed. "So real." Grabbing my phone, I dialed Alex. "Hey, Gwyn had another run-in with the fucking asshole. Can I bring her over? I think she might need stitches."

"I was just leaving. I'll grab a suture kit and stop by on my way home."

"Thanks." I looked at Gwyn, who was still staring at the check. "He'll be here in ten minutes."

"Where did you get this kind of money?"

"I sold my company."

She picked her head up. "Seriously?"

I smiled, taking the check out of her hand and putting it back in my wallet. "Yep. That company ruined my relationship with Ashley. Well, at least, I think it did, and I am in no way going to risk it ruining this."

"You sold your company for me?"

"Yes and no. I sold it for me. I was done, burnt out. Tired of the life. Come on, let's get your face washed up." She followed me into the bathroom and sat on the counter while I cleaned the blood off her face. "I'm pissed he did this to you. Now I can't kiss you."

She giggled. "I can't believe you knocked him out with one punch. You're a badass."

"I box for fun."

"Maybe I should take up boxing."

"How about you let me beat the shit out of him, and you keep your face away from his fist?" That sent her into a fit of giggles.

"You are such a man, defending the helpless woman."

"I would never consider you helpless." The knock on the door pulled me away from her. It was Alex. "Come on, she's in the bathroom."

I stood in the doorway while he put two stitches near her eye. "What the fuck is wrong with this guy?" He looked at me. "I hope you kicked his ass."

Gwyn laughed. "One punch, and he was lying on his back. Knocked his ass out."

Alex laughed. "Yep, sounds like you. All right, you should be good. Wait until tomorrow to get it wet. I have to go. Alice and I are going out to dinner."

I walked him out. When I came back, she was unpacking some of her things. I changed into sweats and went to watch some television. When she finished, she came out and laid on my chest. "I have to go to dinner tonight, and I don't want to go."

"Do you want me to go with you?"

"I think I might. I don't think I want to face my father right now. Jaycen, why do men hit?"

I held her tight. "I don't know, Angel. I just don't know."

"I'm so sorry that I brought all this drama into your life." Her voice was groggy.

"I'm not. I'm glad you are here. I couldn't be happier that I met you."

She giggled. "You married me."

"I would do it again. It was the best decision of my life."

"You think?"

"I know."

"I'm tired, Jaycen. Really tired."

"You sleep for a bit. I'll hold you."

"Mmm, I love you." She kissed my chest.

"I love you, too, Angel." I lay there with my broken and destroyed woman in my arms. My heart had never hurt so badly for someone before. I had to find a way to get her away from him, to get him to stop. I closed my eyes, listening to her breathe. In seven days, this woman had become my life. The only thing I wanted was to be with her. I woke to hear her whisper my name. "What's wrong."

"Someone's at the door."

"I don't know who it could be. No one knows I'm here except for Alex," I whispered but didn't move. The knock came again.

"Are you going to answer it?"

"Do you want me to?" She shook her head. "Like I said, no one knows I'm here, and no one can get in the elevator."

"He knows people. He could make them open it."

I felt her body tense up. "No, sweetheart, it isn't him."

We laid there, me holding her, wanting her to calm down. She was shaking. The knocking stopped, and slowly, she calmed down. "What time is it?"

Reaching for my phone, I swiped it on. "Five." I noticed I had a few missed calls and some texts. I set it back on the table. I didn't care who'd called.

"We should get ready."

"Where's dinner?"

"The Seasons. You sure you don't mind coming with me?"

"To be honest, not that I want to sound like a possessive bastard, but there is no way you are leaving this room without me."

"Thank you." She climbed off me and walked toward the bedroom. "Hey, there's a note on the floor." She moved to the door, picking it up. I got up and walked over to her. "It has your name on it." She handed it to me. "I'm going to get ready." I kissed her on the temple.

Opening the envelope, it said. *Call me. Emergency. Alex.*

I turned and grabbed my phone. Swiping it on, I saw six missed calls from him and two messages. I dialed his number.

"Jesus, Jay, I've been trying to call you. There's been an accident." My heart stopped.

"What happened?"

"I'm not sure. I'm at the hospital. Ashley's been hurt. Someone beat the fuck out of her. She's in the operating room. Man, you've got to get over here."

Looking at the bedroom door, I told him, "I can't. Just call me when you find out what happened. I have something I need to do, and then I'll come by. But I can't right now."

"Jay, what the hell? You were going to marry this girl."

"It's been over for a long time, Alex. I can't come right now. I'll come when I get done."

"All right, but answer your damn phone, will you?"

"I will. Thanks for calling."

Shaking my head, I turned the ringer up and put the phone down. I walked into the bedroom and found Gwyn standing in one of the bra and panty sets I bought her, and fuck if she didn't look fantastic. I whistled at her. "Mighty fine woman. Mighty fine. So, I'm wearing a suit?"

"Thank you, and yes."

Walking into the closet, I opened the top drawer. Reaching in, I pulled out the box with the bracelet, then I smiled and got dressed. She was waiting for me in the living room and stood up when I walked out. Fuck if she didn't look beautiful. Reaching into my pocket, I pulled the box out. "I have something for you."

She smiled. "You bought me a present? Jaycen, you don't need to buy me anything."

"I know, but I wanted you to have it." I handed her the box. Her eyes filled with tears when she opened it.

"Oh my God." Her eyes shot up to mine.

"I saw you admiring it. Think of it as a wedding present." I took it out of the box and put it on her wrist. "It's perfect. "

"You're crazy." Her smile, those dimples did me in. "Thank you."

Wrapping my hand around her neck, I kissed her. I really wanted to take her dress off and make love to her, but we had somewhere we needed to be. "I love you."

"I love you."

I took her hand, and we headed out. I had my driver meet us in the garage. We sat holding hands on the drive, and when we walked in, she excused herself to use the restroom. I followed behind her and waited in the hall.

"Jay?" I turned to see Ally walking up to me. She was moving slowly.

"Hey, beautiful. What are you doing here?" When I hugged her, I felt her body tighten, and she winced. "You all right?"

She smiled. "Yeah, I fell down the stairs this morning. What are you doing here?"

I wiggled my eyebrows at her. "I'm on a date."

She smiled. "No kidding. I'm glad. Does Caden know?"

"Nope. What are you doing here?"

"Same, but with my parents. You should stop by and say hi."

"I'll do that."

She patted my arm and walked away. A few minutes later, Gwyn came up to me. "I heard you talking to someone." She slipped her arm in mine.

"Yeah, my friend's girlfriend. They are having dinner here tonight as well."

"Oh, so I get to meet your friend?"

"I suppose you do. Shall we go?"

"I don't want to do this. If my grandmother wasn't here, I wouldn't be here at all. How does my makeup look?"

I looked at her. She had tried to cover the bruise forming on her eye. "It looks fine."

We headed into the restaurant. Moving to the back of the room, I saw Caden sitting next to Ally. Across the table was the Police Commissioner. My feet stopped moving as Gwyn approached the table. Caden stood up and hugged her. When the man with his back to me stood, Gwyn backed up, and I heard her. "What the fuck are you doing here?" I think I was in shock.

"Watch your mouth, young lady," her father growled out.

Gavin moved from his spot and pulled out the chair next to him. It was the only one at the table. Gwyn stepped back, and Caden grabbed her arm. She tried to pull away from him, but he had a fucking hold of her. My feet were moving.

"No!" I shouted. "Get your fucking hands off her."

Caden's face said it all. "Jay? What the hell are you doing here?"

I pushed him away from her and pulled her behind me. "Don't ever touch her again." My eyes moved to Ally, then back to Caden. I stepped back, pulling Gwyn in front of me. "Ally is your sister?" She just stood there looking at me. "Gwyn?"

"He's your friend?" Her eyes moved to Caden. "You're his friend?"

"How the hell do you know each other?" Caden asked.

"She's my wife."

"He's my husband."

Her father stood up. "What?"

I happened to look at her mother, who had a small smile on her face. Then my eyes moved to Gavin, who was still standing. I happened to notice his hands; his knuckles were bruised. Then my gaze moved back to Caden. "You hurt her?" My eyes looked at Ally. "He beats you?" The horror on her face told me what I already knew. "You son of a bitch." I swung. I couldn't help it. "I've known you my whole life, and you turn out to be some low life piece of shit who beats his girlfriend?" Turning, I looked at her father. "He's just like you. Who beats his wife, beats his children." He went to open his mouth. "Don't bother denying it. I've seen the pictures." My eyes moved to Gavin. "She is my wife; she is nothing to you. I don't give a shit who you think you are, but you don't know who I am. My name is Jaycen Ashford." I watched his eyes get big; her father sat down. "Her name is Gwyn Ashford. You touch her again, and I will make sure you don't get out of prison until it's time to bury you. If you think you can beat me, then bring it, fucker. This is the last time I am going to tell you. Do. Not. Touch. My. Wife. Do you understand me?" He gave me a look, and I stepped forward. "Do you understand me?"

"Yeah."

Caden was standing off to the side. "You and I are not friends anymore. I can't be friends with someone who hurts women." Then I looked at Ally. "He spent the night in a sex club downtown with Gavin last night. The place is called Maxi's. If you marry him, you're the fool, but hear me; Gwyn and I will not be there."

Her father stood again. "Wait just a minute. You do not tell me what to do. Do you have any idea who I am?"

I laughed. "You are a low life piece of shit. I don't care if you are the Police Commissioner. If you hit your wife or daughters again, you will no longer be the Police Commissioner. The mayor's daughter is a client of mine, so go ahead and try me. I have the pictures to prove you're the biggest asshole on the planet." I looked at her mother and grandmother. "Ladies, I apologize for my rudeness and my foul mouth. I'm sorry it isn't under better circumstances that we meet. You have a lovely evening." I took Gwyn's hand and moved over to Gavin. Leaning in, I had to stop myself from smiling when he flinched. "If I find out it was you that beat Ashley so bad that she is in surgery, they won't find your body." I moved away, looking at Caden, shaking my head, and wrapped my arm around Gwyn. We walked out, both of us with our heads held high.

Gwyn

When he shouted, my eyes turned to him. He was fast as he got me away from Caden. I froze when he said he was Caden's friend. What the fuck? His words were flying in all directions. I looked at my mom and grandmother, who both sat there with small smiles on their faces, their eyes on him. It warmed my heart to see my mother happy with my choice of a man. He was going to town on everyone. It was when he punched his friend in the face and ended their friendship that I needed to hide my smile. When he moved us to Gavin, my body began to shake, but the calming hand of my mother squeezing my hand made my heart warm. He wrapped his arm around my waist, and we walked through the restaurant with our heads held high.

We didn't wait for his car. We got in a cab that was waiting at the curb. I turned my head to look out the window. I couldn't wipe the smile off my face, and I knew he was pissed. So, we just sat there holding hands.

Jaycen

I wasn't sure what to do, what to say to her. I just bulldozed my way through her life. Fucking Caden! Why hadn't I connected the dots before? The things he'd said over the years, and the times when Ally couldn't make it to dinner. He was beating the fuck out of her. God, I was so pissed off. I looked at Gwyn, who was looking out the window. I can see her reflection and the small smile on her face, so maybe I hadn't fuck things up. We pulled up to the hotel, then I paid the cab driver and got out. Turning, I reached for her hand, and when she placed hers in mine, I didn't feel her shaking. As she stood, she looked right in my eyes. We didn't say a word as we walked through the lobby. When we got upstairs, I said, "Can you change your clothes? We need to go somewhere." She nodded. We changed and left again.

Walking through the hospital, I found Alex sitting in a waiting room. When he saw me, he stood, he had tears streaming down his face. I hugged him, and he whispered in my ear, "She didn't make it."

My heart hurt. I hugged him tighter, the tears falling on my cheeks. "What the hell happened?"

When we separated, Alex smiled at Gwyn, and we sat. "The police were here earlier. They said they found her in an alley a few blocks from the Seasons. She had been raped and beaten. Her head had been slammed into the ground so many times that her brain swelled, and they couldn't stop it."

"Do they know who did it?"

"Apparently, more than a few people saw the guy as he ran away. He was wearing a grey suit."

My eyes moved to look at Gwyn. Fucking Gavin Highland was wearing a grey suit. But there wasn't any blood on it, not that I could see, but then again, I saw red from the blind fury. "Do you have a contact for the police?" He handed me a card. "Where are her personal belongings?"

"That's what I'm waiting for."

I wanted to tell him about Caden, but now was not the time. Gwyn didn't say a word; she just sat there with her eyes glued to me. I couldn't help but wonder if she was waiting for a reaction from me. We didn't say another word. I'm not sure how long we sat, but I held her hand the entire time. Finally, a woman walked over with a bag and looked at Alex. "These are the personal effects for Ashley Maxus." I watched as Alex stood and thanked her. After taking the bag, he turned and handed it to me.

I hugged my friend and thanked him. Taking Gwyn's hand, we left the hospital. I had my driver take me to John's house. Looking at my watch, I saw it was going on nine-thirty. When we pulled up to the gate, I got out of the car and pushed the buzzer.

"Jaycen Ashford to see Mr. Reed," I said into the intercom.

"Come right up," the voice said. I stood there looking at the gates as they opened, then at the car with Gwyn in the backseat. My job now was to make her safe, to keep her safe. I was in love with her, and she was my wife.

I got back in the car, and she grabbed my hand, squeezing it hard. I knew she was afraid of what I was about to do, but I was done. Someone killed Ashley, and as much as I didn't want to be with her, no one deserved to die like that.

The car stopped near the door, at the curve in the circular driveway, and we got out. Taking the bag with me, I didn't let go of Gwyn's hand. If there were no words said, at least she felt me next to her, keeping her safe. We were shown into John's office, and he was sitting behind his desk. When we walked in, he smiled at me and moved to stand, but when he saw Gwyn, his expression changed. He had already been informed of the events that took place this evening. "Jay, good to see you. What can I do for you?"

"Well, John, that depends on you. That depends on whether I'm correct in the idea that you are an upstanding, honest man, or if you are in the pocket of some low life asshole." He gave me a nervous chuckle. "Someone murdered Ashley this evening, and I believe I know who it was and their reasoning behind it. But what I don't know is if you are going to do the right thing here, or if you are going to cover it up and let the fucking scumbags get away with it."

His eyes moved from me to Gwyn. "Gwendolyn."

She smiled at him. "John."

I think I might have been in a bit of shock. "You two know one another?"

"Jay, her father is the Police Commissioner. Of course, I know her."

"Actually, John, he's not my father. I think he murdered my father so he could be with my mother. I can't prove it, but I can prove that he and Gavin Highland are dirty, among other things."

He tilted his head. "He's not your father?"

She shook her head, squeezing my hand. "Bill Knight is my father. He died when I was four, murdered by some drug addict. Tom was his partner. Two years later, Tom married my mom and insisted that we go by his last name, but he never adopted us."

I looked at John. "Gwyn is my wife, which goes against what Gavin Highland wants. He nearly killed her a little over a week ago; there are plenty of witnesses. He attacked her today, as you can see. Her body is covered in healing bruises, and her hair has been ripped out to the point of balding."

He looked confused. "I was told by Tom that she is mentally unstable, has been most of her life. Wild with disciplinary problems. That you, my dear, have been in and out of treatment facilities. That you've attacked Gavin on more than one occasion. Are you telling me that's not true?"

I felt her squeeze my hand again. I think we both saw it at the same time because she moved just as I did, picking up the Time magazine on the table next to a chair. She laid it down on the desk in front of him. "This is mine. The article is about me. When Gavin beat on me, I would leave. I'd go on photo shoots. It's the only time I could because he wouldn't ever let me do anything that wasn't his idea. Those photographs are mine. The reporter will tell you that she interviewed me. I am not crazy; I just refuse to allow them to beat me down anymore. I think Gavin killed Ashley, maybe not on purpose, but to get Jaycen away from me so he could kidnap me. He's been trying to get me alone since that night at the Jewel. His intention is to kill me. I know it now."

I watched John process everything. "John, I know you are a good man. We've known each other for a very long time. Do you think I am capable of any of this? Do you think I could hurt anyone? I didn't do this to her. I'm trying to save my wife. Now, are you going to help us and do the right thing, or are you going to protect these bastards and let them kill her as well?"

He sat there looking from me to Gwyn. I felt her hand squeeze mine again. I turned to look at her. "I told you that no one would help us. Come on. This is a waste of time."

I nodded to her, and we turned, making it to the door before he said anything. "Jay?" I turned. "You have proof of this?"

"We do."

"I'm going to need it."

I nodded, and we walked out. Not a word was said on our way back to the hotel, but my hand never left hers. When we walked into the room, I closed the door and leaned against it while pulling her into my embrace. "I'm so fucking scared he's going to get to you," I whispered.

"Thank you for what you did tonight. When you said you knew Caden, I thought you were like them. But then you stood up to them for me, and for my sister."

Looking at her, my heart grew more for this woman than I ever imagined possible. My fingers wrapped around her neck, pulling her to my mouth. It was a frantic kiss, a kiss that scared the shit out of me. The adrenalin pumping through my body took control. I could feel both of us shaking. Pulling back, our breaths were rushed like we'd just ran five miles. I put my forehead on hers. "I won't let them hurt you again."

Her eyes filled with tears. "He killed her. I'm so sorry, Jaycen."

I couldn't do anything but nod. I felt the loss of Ashley; she'd been a big part of my life at one time, and I had cared for her. No one deserved that. "Thank you, Angel." Her arms wrapped around me, and she held me.

"We need to send everything to John right now. I think, when we are done, we need to leave." Her words were mumbled against my chest.

"Do you think it's wise to run?"

"You told them who you were. They'll know where we are staying." She pulled away from me. "We can't stay here."

"You might be right. I think I know where we can go. Let's pack up. Can you send copies of everything you have to John?"

"If you pack, I'll log on and send it all."

"Deal."

We both moved to the bedroom. I grabbed our suitcases and started packing. "Jaycen, I think we can leave the camping gear. I don't think we should leave until this is over."

She was right. I was nearly done when she smiled at me. "It's done." Her voice was shaky.

I went to her, pulling her off the bed. "It'll be all right."

"I never thought I would do this. I'm going to destroy two people."

"They could both be murders, so we are doing the right thing."

"Let's get out of here." She pulled away. Going into the closet, she finished packing her things. After grabbing her camera bags and her computer, she looked at me. "I'm ready."

"Leave the phones here." We set our phones on the table next to the bed.

I never knew why I bought a car. I only drove every once in a while, but I was glad I had it. My driver took us back to my apartment. When we got to the car, she stood there looking at it. "I had a tracker on my car." She set her stuff down and laid on the ground.

"What are you doing?"

She giggled. "Well, you saw the burner phones in a spy movie. Holy shit."

"What?" I got down on my hands and knees. "What did you find?"

She started scooting out. "This." She handed me a box of some kind with a flashing red light on it. "What is it?"

"I'm not sure but come on. We aren't driving this car." I helped her up, and we left, walking out to the street. I put my hand up and grabbed a cab. Neither of us said a word. "Can you take us to Midway, please?" She looked at me, and I winked.

I rented a car at the airport, and we drove, heading out of the city. I pulled into a hotel and checked us in, but we didn't go to our room. We just went out the side of the building and grabbed a cab. I told the driver where to take us. When we got out, we took our bags and walked.

"I'm not used to this super-spy stuff." She smiled.

I laughed. "Not super-spy shit. The city has cameras everywhere. Your dad is the police and can track us like that. The car rental went on my credit card, and they can track that. I'm sure it's low-jacked with a tracker, so I couldn't drive us here. Checking into the hotel will make them believe we are there. We took the cab here, but here isn't where we are going."

She busted out laughing. "Who are you?"

I stopped, let go of the bags, and pulled her into my arms. I was pissed that her lip was split. "I am your husband. It's my job to protect you."

She was still giggling. "Such a manly man you are." She play-punched my chest.

"Fucking right, I am." My thumb ran across her lip. "I'm so pissed he did this to you."

"Come on. It's late, and I'm exhausted." She let me go, and we continued our walk. Twenty minutes later, I turned us into a drive-way. "This is nice." I nodded. As we moved up the long driveway, the trees blocked our view, and I guided her around the house to the back door. "What's wrong with the front door?"

I just smiled. "He'll turn on the front porch light, and it's late."

She just giggled as I knocked on the door. "Hey, they have a pool down there."

"Yep, and a pool house."

A few minutes later, the light turned on, and Alex opened the door. "Jay, what the hell are you doing here?"

"Long story, but can we come in?"

"Of course. I didn't hear a car. How'd you get here?"

We left our bags outside. "We walked," Gwyn told him.

Alex moved out of the way, and we walked into the kitchen just as Alice was walking in from the hall. "Oh my goodness, Jay." She ran up and threw herself in my arms. "I am so sorry about Ashley," she said into my neck. I hugged her hard. I hadn't seen her in a long time.

"Thank you."

We pulled apart, and Alex introduced her to Gwyn. I watched Alice embrace her and then smile at me. "What brings you here this time of the night?"

I looked at Alex. "We need a place to hide. I was kind of hoping we could stay in your pool house for a few days."

"What's going on, Jay?"

Gwyn spoke. "The man who we believe killed Ashley is the same man who did this to my face and the rest of my body."

Alex's eyes shot to me. "Seriously?"

"Yes, and it's a long story, but we need a place to stay for a while."

Alice smiled at me. "Come on. I'll make some tea."

We sat at the table and told Alex and Alice the whole story. "You're married?" Alice smiled. "Oh, Jay, I'm so happy for you. I just can't believe that about Caden and Ally."

"Oh, believe it. She is my sister, and he is a mean bastard," Gwyn said.

"Until this settles down, we need a safe place to stay, and I was hoping we could crash in your pool house."

"Of course, you can." Alice reached across the table and grabbed my hand. "Whatever you need, Jay. You know that."

"Thank you." I squeezed her hand then looked at Alex. "You can't tell Caden we are here or that you've seen us."

"He already called me. I told him about Ashley and that the last time I saw you was at the hospital."

"Keep it that way. What did he say about Ashley?"

"Oh, he sounded pissed. Very upset. He told me what happened at the restaurant, about you punching him in the face, and that you told him you weren't friends anymore." I shook my head. "He also said that they called off the wedding. Ally's mom and grandmother forbade her from marrying him."

Gwyn reached up and wiped the tear off her cheek. I wrapped my arm around her, pulling her to my chest, and kissed her head. I knew it was a tear of joy. Her sister was safe now. "Listen, do you mind if we crash? It's been a crazy day."

"Come on." Alex stood. "I took a few days off, so I'll be home. There's an intercom from the house. I'll let you know when it's safe to come up. Just lay low back there. You're safe here."

"Thanks." I hugged Alice and told her goodnight. We walked out, grabbed our things, and Alex took us down to the pool house.

"Try not to turn on the lights."

"We are just going to crash. Thanks, man. We'll talk tomorrow." I hugged him, and he left. I locked the door and watched as Gwyn looked around.

"Jaycen, is there a bed in here?" She looked exhausted.

I took her hand and led her to the small room in the back. She used the bathroom and came out naked, then crawled on the bed. I followed her, wrapping myself around her. She cried in my chest, her whole body shaking. We didn't talk. I just held on to her.

CHAPTER TWELVE

GWYN

I'd been quiet all night, ever since he hit Caden. I just didn't know what to say or what to do. No one had ever stuck up for me, fought for me, or cared enough about me to do so. When we heard about his ex, my heart hurt for him. I knew he felt bad, and I knew he had to be upset about it, especially hearing the news that she didn't make it. I felt his sorrow, the way his body slumped in anguish. But he held strong for me.

So, I laid there in his arms, crying my eyes out for all that had happened, and he held me. I pulled myself together and sat up. He rolled onto his back, putting his arm behind his head. "What's wrong?" His voice sounded so kind.

"I'm so sorry about Ashley."

He put his hand on my leg. "Thank you."

"Jaycen, what you did tonight... your friend... Gavin, my father. There just aren't words. When you saved me, I just thought you were this beautiful stranger who was a rich asshole. But over the last eight days, you've changed my life. You've stood up for me time and again. You are so much more than a rich asshole. There aren't words I can find to tell you how grateful I am, how much I appreciate what you have done and what you are doing." He sat up, his hand wrapping around my neck, his thumb brushing along my cheek. "You are so much more, you..."

He leaned in and kissed me. "You don't need words, Angel. I fell in love with you that first night. I would do anything; I will do anything to keep you safe. This will end, and we will be happy."

"I am happy right now, as crazy as all of this is. I haven't been happier."

"I'm worried that, when all this excitement dies down and you are finally safe, you won't need me anymore." His words shocked me.

I leaned into his chest, laying us down. "I will always need you. I'll always need this." His arms wrapped around me. I laid my head on his chest. "I love you," I whispered.

"I love you," he whispered back.

My eyes closed, and my body relaxed for probably the first time in days. I hadn't ever felt so safe.

Jaycen

The remarkable quality of this woman in my arms had my mind numb. Not that I had a fucking clue how any of this mess was going to turn out. I just knew that, no matter what, I was not leaving her to do it alone. I had enough money for us to hide for a long time. When her body completely relaxed, my heart calmed down. She was sound asleep on my chest, one leg resting between mine and the other wrapped around my thigh. God, she was perfect.

I closed my eyes, inhaling her scent. My mind closed itself off, and I finally crashed.

Waking to the feeling of her tongue on my nipple, my eyes slowly opened to see she was enjoying herself. My cock, which was already semi-hard, hardened more. When she realized I was awake, she pushed my arms up the bed, over my head. She brought her mouth up to mine, her kiss bringing me to a total erection. Pulling back, she smiled at me. "Keep your hands there, and don't touch me."

I chuckled. "That's going to be hard, Angel."

"Please, don't touch me." She smiled, kissing me.

She pulled back and sunk her teeth into the head of my cock, and I lost it. "Oh, fuck." I felt my legs push up on the bed, my stomach tighter than it should be. The fucking orgasm that blew through my body shook me to my core. My hands hurt from grabbing the spindles in the headboard. I could hear the creak as I struggled not to grab her.

When she finished, she knelt on the bed, looking at me. "Thank you." My hands slowly released the spindles and moved to touch her, but she shook her head. "No. I want you to know how you make me feel every time you touch me."

"Angel, I need to touch you."

She shook her head. "Just think about me for the rest of the day. When this day is over, I want you to fuck me." She smiled as a blush washed over her body. Her voice was so soft as she whispered. "Hard."

It was the hardest thing in the world not to grab her and kiss her. I smiled. "I love you, beautiful." As my eyes closed, I felt her move off the bed, and then the shower was running. A few minutes later, she came out with a towel wrapped around her head. I got up and took a shower. We dressed and sat looking at one another.

"I wonder if John got everything," I said.

"I don't know the WIFI password here, so I can't check to see if he wrote back. But I do have these." She reached in her bag and pulled out the burner phones.

"Smartest woman I know." Taking one from her, I called his office. "John, it's Jaycen Ashford."

"This is some pretty damning evidence you've sent me. I've already started an internal investigation. Gavin Highland has been fired and arrested. He isn't going anywhere. He was, in fact, identified as the man who beat Ashley to death, so he will be tried for her murder." My eyes moved to Gwyn. "As for the Commissioner, well, he has been put on administrative leave, pending my investigation, but if all of this is true, he will at some point be arrested and tried for the murder of Gwyn's father and the countless other crimes he's committed. Well done, Jay. Thank you for this."

"Does this mean we are safe? Can we go home?"

"I think you should stay lost for a few more days. Tom is a violent man, and his daughter just took him down. Maybe stay hidden and under the radar until this is finished and I know what to charge him with. Tell Gwyn I have her mother and sister in protective custody. I'm sorry to tell you this, but I believe Caden McGraw might be involved as well. At least, that's what my preliminary reports indicate."

"Thanks, John. I'll give you a call in a day or two."

"No problem. Watch the news."

I disconnected the phone and turned it off, then pulled the battery out of it. Gwyn sat there with fear on her face. "Gavin is in jail for Ashley's murder. Your dad has been put on administrative leave. John has your mom and sister in protective custody. He thinks Caden is involved. He suggested we stay lost for a few days."

Before I finished the first sentence, the tears began falling from her eyes. I wanted to touch her, but she made me promise not to touch her. "Thank you, Jaycen, for all of this. I will spend the rest of my life in your debt."

"No, Angel, there is no debt to be paid. I am your husband. It's part of my job description. Let me touch you. I need to touch you."

She shook her head. "Can we eat?"

I nodded, looking at my watch. "It's one-thirty. Jesus, we slept the whole night and day. Come on. Let's go eat." As I reached for the handle to the door, the intercom clicked on. It was Alice's voice.

"Cops," she said. Neither of us moved. She left the transmitter turned on. We just stood there, looking at each other as we listened to the cops interviewing Alex and Alice. They wanted to talk about Caden. Jesus Christ, John wasn't kidding. What the fuck did he do? There was no mention of Gwyn or me.

"Well, thank you for your time. If you can think of anything else, here is my card."

We waited for Alice to give us the okay.

After the all-clear, we walked into the main house, and Alex stood there looking at me. "What the fuck did he do?"

"I don't know, but I talked to John. He said that the investigation is in full swing, and Caden is part of this mess, but he never said why."

"Here, come sit down. Let me get you something to eat," Alice said.

"Let me help." Gwyn moved from my side.

Alex leaned in. "Do you think he's been doing illegal shit?"

"Well, beating the shit out of Ally on a regular basis is illegal. I still can't believe that. Some of the things he has said to me just make my skin crawl."

Alice and Gwyn came back with sandwiches, and we sat and ate. "I'll go shopping and get you two some things. Let's make a list, so you have food out there. I would imagine with you being newlyweds, you would rather be alone."

I laughed. "Thanks, Alice. We are still getting to know one another."

When we finished, Gwyn smiled at Alex and Alice. "I really appreciate you hiding us, and I don't want to be rude, but we haven't slept much in the past week or so, and no, it's not a sex thing. So much has happened, and well, I'm just exhausted and want to sleep. Thank you again for helping me, but I'm just going to go back to bed."

I smiled at her. "Come on, Angel. I'll go with you. Alice, whatever you normally get for you and Alex in the food department is fine. I'll come up later and get it from you, after we sleep for a bit."

Alice hugged us both, and we went back to the pool house. The minute the door was closed, she was moving toward the bedroom, peeling her clothes off. "Now that we are really safe for a bit, I think everything has caught up with me. I really am tired, Jaycen. Will you come and sleep with me?"

Pushing off the door, I followed her like a lost little puppy. Climbing in bed and wrapping my arms around her was the calm in this shit storm that we needed.

~

Gwyn

Sitting there listening to them talk about Gavin and Caden made my stomach sore. I just couldn't shake the fear that I was with someone who was so violent, violent enough to beat that beautiful woman to death. Looking at Jaycen, I couldn't even imagine how he was feeling, and he kept it inside because he didn't want me to see his pain. I wasn't sure if that was a good thing.

I was truly exhausted and tried to sleep, but I couldn't. He was wrapped around me, making me feel safe, but what was I doing for him? My body moved away from his, and I sat up, wrapping the sheet around me.

"What's the matter, Angel?" His voice was always so kind and considerate.

"You. You're what's the matter."

"What do you mean?" I could see his body tense. He thought he'd done something wrong. I liked that he worried about upsetting me, but this wasn't what I wanted. I wanted freedom.

"Please, don't take this the wrong way. I might not be able to get it out with the right words, and that's only because my thoughts were basically suppressed. Before, when I voiced them, I was hurt. But you are not being honest or truthful with me, and in a sense, that's not fair."

He sat up, reaching his hand out for me, and I moved back, shaking my head. The hurt in his eyes was very evident as he pulled his hand away. "Please, Angel, tell me what you are thinking." I could hear the pain in his voice.

"I've lived most of my life with my senses hyperaware, so I can feel people. You are not being truthful. I can feel it. You are so kind and loving, so caring toward me, protecting me, wanting me to be safe, that you are not allowing me to feel you completely. In the beginning, I wasn't aware of it simply because you were so kind to me. After yesterday, everything became clear to me. It was as if all this fog lifted."

His face, his eyes told me that he was scared and confused. "I don't think I understand what you are saying."

"I have to assume because I don't know for sure, but you got the call about Ashley before we left for dinner. I heard you on the phone, saying you couldn't go." He nodded. "But you didn't show me any distress about you getting that news. Instead, you gave me this beautiful bracelet." I held up my arm. "Dinner happened, and then we went to the hospital where you found out she died. She was murdered. You knew that Gavin did it, but you were so closed off about it. Then at John's house, you were so calm, so perfect. The only thing I got from you was a squeeze of your hand. I know you are trying to protect me and keep me safe, which I am grateful for, but you are keeping me in the dark when it comes to your emotions. I'm sure you think you are protecting me, but you're not. You're hurting me, making me feel that I can't completely trust you." I felt myself start to tear up, but I wasn't going to cry. "I'm not a weak woman. I'm stronger than you give me credit for. Please, don't get me wrong here; I love that you are so protective, but I want to be the same for you. I feel like I am taking and not giving you what you need. Jaycen, you loved her. You cared for her so much so that you bought her an engagement ring. I wasn't around for the initial pain of her cheating on you, but you can't sit here and tell me that her death doesn't affect you."

He sat looking at me, and I could see his internal struggle. I didn't say another word. I watched his hand move a few times and knew he was going to touch me, but he stopped himself. We sat looking at each for a long time. The crackle of the intercom in the living space interrupted us.

"Jay, turn on the TV."

He turned away, grabbed the remote, and turned on the television. I didn't look away from him.

We interrupt with a breaking news story.

Gavin Highland was found dead in his cell just a few minutes ago, an apparent suicide.

Relief washed through me, cleansing my soul. As much pain as the man had caused me, I knew I still shouldn't feel this way.

Police Commissioner Thomas James has been arrested in the twenty-three-year-old murder of his partner, William Knight, along with charges of accepting bribes, extortion, and money laundering.

Caden McGraw of McGraw Industries has been arrested for embezzlement, racketeering, and money laundering.

I didn't take my eyes off Jaycen. He showed no emotion whatsoever concerning his lifelong friend. I couldn't help but wonder if he was more broken than me. I felt relief and a sense of peace now that I knew they were gone. It was time to pick up the pieces of my life, heal, and live again. The only question in my mind was whether I could do it with the man in front of me. He was so emotionally closed off for whatever reasons.

He turned off the TV, his eyes moving to me. "He's..." I shook my head. He wasn't going to make this about me and my safety. I got up and put on my clothes. He just sat there and watched me. Picking up my backpack and my camera bags, I leaned in and kissed him. I knew what I had to do, what I always did to survive. I needed to go make peace with what had happened.

"I think I will always love you, but I can't be with you if you won't let me in. You want all that I am, and well, I want the same from you. When you figure out how to give it to me, you know where to find me." I kissed him again and walked out. He didn't chase me. He didn't try to stop me, so I knew he felt what I'd said to him. My heart hurt so bad. I wanted him. I wanted to love him.

Jaycen

The tears fell from my eyes as I sat on the bed paralyzed as she kissed me and walked out the door. Every fucking word she said to me was the truth. I couldn't even defend myself. My heart was pounding like a racehorse's hooves on race day. I sat there for so long, just looking at the door and hoping she would come back, hoping she would try harder, but she didn't return. Lying back, I cried myself to sleep. I wanted to throw up, but she was right. I didn't know how to share my feelings. She was right; I wanted everything from her, but I wasn't willing to give her the same.

When I woke, I got dressed and called a cab. I needed to head back to the city and get my wife. She was so important to me. I think I forgot that she didn't need me to survive. I had the cab take me to the hotel, and then I headed over to her apartment. I wasn't letting her go.

I knocked on her door, but there was no answer, so I sat and waited. I wasn't leaving without her. I just sat there, thinking about the words she'd left me with. For hours I sat, knocking every now and then, but nothing. I got up and put my hand on her door. "I love you, Angel."

Defeated and gutted, I left. When I walked into the hotel room, I went straight to my bed. I didn't even bother taking my clothes off; I was in so much pain. When I woke up, I was pretty sure days had passed. I used the bathroom, brushed my teeth, and then changed my clothes. I was going back to her place; I was going to fight for her. When I walked out to leave, I saw her shoes on the floor. Spinning around, my eyes searched the room. It was empty. They landed on the doorway into the other bedroom. I felt like a zombie as I moved toward the door. When I crossed the threshold, there she was, sleeping. I wanted to scream, but I just slid down the door and sat on the floor, my tears falling.

She said I would know where to find her. Never did I think she would be here. My eyes pinned to her face; it was nearly cleared of bruises now, but her lip was still puffy and her eye a bit purple. She rolled over; her back was nearly it's soft pink color. My beautiful wife was coming back to herself. I didn't move; I couldn't move. She sat up, swinging her feet over the edge of the bed, and just sat there.

"I'm not sure how to give you that part of me. I've never done it before."

"This won't work, Jaycen, unless you give me all of you. Just start with how you feel about what happened with Ashley. Once you start, it will just come. I want to be your wife. I want to love you, but I can't completely. Only you can do that for me. I can't make you do it."

"I was so scared when Alex told me what happened. I was afraid that, if you saw my fear, you would think I didn't care about you. So, I buried it, just like I bury everything that makes my life difficult. I'm afraid that if I show real emotion, true emotion, it will be used against me."

"Is that how you feel about me?"

She didn't turn around; she just sat there with her back to me.

"No, that's what's so real about us. I know you wouldn't. Like you, everyone else tore me to shreds, and because I'm a man, I needed to hide it, to keep it tucked away so I would never look weak. Men aren't supposed to be weak."

"You know that's bullshit."

I put my head down. "When everything happened at the Seasons, I was already to the brim of fear. Caden has been my friend most of my life, and he turned out to be this horrible man. The betrayal I felt was so foreign to me that I needed to just put it away. I can't, nor do I want to feel anything for him. Just having the knowledge that he hurt Ally like that for so many years makes me sick. He was my friend."

"He is still your friend."

I shook my head, even though she couldn't see me. "I don't want him to be my friend. How did I not know those things about him? How fucking self-involved am I that I didn't notice he was beating her up, and that he was in so deep he could never get out?"

"Well, you told me that you were burnt out. You were so busy building your business that you lost Ashley over it. How were you supposed to see that your friend was in trouble? Tell me how you felt at the hospital."

"It nearly brought me to my knees. I felt it deep in my heart, but I had to hide that from you. I didn't want you to think she mattered to me."

"See, you are cheating me out of that deep emotion inside of you. I'm not a jealous or petty woman, Jaycen. I know she mattered to you, and I know she hurt you. You know how I know? Because if you did it to me, I don't think I would recover. I love you. I want a life with you. Not because you are rich, or gorgeous, or that you saved me. But because I feel you deep in my soul, deep in my heart. Like you've been there my whole life. I can't give all of me to you unless you give all of you to me. I came here because I promised myself, I wouldn't sleep away from you again. You are my husband."

"Angel, please tell me if it was enough?"

"For now, it's more than you have given me. So, for now, it's enough. You need to trust me, Jaycen. You need to trust that I would never use your emotions against you. You trust me with all your money, but I want the same with your emotions, with your heart. Can you give me that?"

"Yes."

She turned and looked at me, sitting on the floor. Her hand lifted off the bed. Slowly, I got off the floor and moved to her. Taking her hand in mine, I sat down next to her. "I don't know how any of this happened, but I am so in love with you, Jaycen. I want a life with you. Do you want the same with me?" She had tears in her eyes.

"I do, Angel. I so do."

He watched her climb back in bed. "Come to bed, Jaycen. I'm so very tired." I took off my clothes and climbed in behind her, wrapping her in my arms. Closing my eyes, we slept.

EPILOGUE

Thomas James was found guilty of murdering Gwyn's father, taking bribes, and racketeering. He was sentenced to life in prison but was murdered three days into his sentence.

Jaycen and Gwyn went to Caden's trial every day and listened to the crimes that he had committed. He pled no contest and was sentenced to fifteen years in prison. When he was escorted out of the courtroom, he looked at his friend and dropped his head in shame.

When it was all over, Jaycen and Gwyn never left one another's side. They traveled all over the world so she could take her photographs. Together, they lived their lives to the fullest. Jaycen learned to trust Gwyn with every thought and every emotion.

They lived a happy life. Two lost souls that had been reunited over time.

More Books by Cin Medley

Broken
One Hundred Acres
Six Months
Beautiful Liar
Is this Life
Justice
Within The Ashes
Secrets
Lyssa's Journey
Lines Crossed
Winter Harbor
Everything She Thought